PRAISE FOR GARRETT LEIGH

"Emotional and brilliant…"

ALL ABOUT ROMANCE

"Tastefully erotic … more smart than smutty…"

PUBLISHERS WEEKLY

"Powerful and compelling…"

FOREWORD REVIEWS

KISS ME AGAIN

GARRETT LEIGH

Editing: Posy Roberts @ bohopress.com

Proofing: Jacque Smith, Anna Martin, Annabelle Jacobs

Cover Art: Garrett Leigh @ blackjazzdesign.com

AUTHOR'S NOTE

Many thanks to **M** for the insight into your life with bipolar and the double round of sensitivity reads. I will use many of your words in the following note: Ludo's experience of bipolar disorder, though heavily influenced by painstaking research, is fictional. It is not, and was never intended to be, *the* experience of bipolar. No opinions expressed in this book should be taken as medical advice. If you are experiencing difficulties with your mental health, please reach out to a healthcare professional.

"Kiss me again, Aidan . . . please?"

ONE

Aidan

"It's two hours, Aidan. Do you have to be a wanker about everything?"

I spare Bernard, my boss, a bored glance. "It's not two hours. That bozo you hired is an epic fuck-up. Whoever takes over has to start all over again. At best, it's a half day."

"So? It's one o'clock."

"I finish at three, mate."

Bernard's glare turns murderous. "I'm asking you to work overtime—two hours, like I said in the first place, at time and a half. Don't mug me off here. Remember you were late on Monday *and* hanging out of your arse yesterday. You owe me a solid."

I owe kind-hearted Bernard far more than that, but I'm not in the mood to spend any longer out in the cold than I absolutely have to, even if I need the money.

Being a prick is easier than giving a shit.

I light a cigarette and ignore Bernard's increasing frustration. Awkward silence never bothers me. Why would it when I've spent most of my life alone?

Bernard sighs. "All right. Double time, and that's my final offer. If that ain't enough for you, I'll do it my damned self."

As if. Bernard is pushing seventy and hasn't been fit enough to scale a tree in years. He's also loaded, so I don't feel all that bad for rinsing an extra fifty quid out of him. "Whatevs. I'll do it. But if I'm not finished by five, I'm leaving anyway."

"Of course you are." Bernard drops a set of keys on the drystone wall I'm lounging against. "Just don't dump the van at the pub again, or I'll have yer balls."

He stomps away, leaving me to finish my smoke in peace.

I don't bother to watch him go. Instead, I stub my fag out and flick it into a nearby bin. *I can't be arsed with this shite.* But I'm already three days late paying rent, and I've spent half my impending wages on tick at the shop. Without this last minute job, I'm pretty much fucked.

The tree that needs felling is in the front garden of one of the nicest houses in Buckbourne. Rich twats that get on my last nerve with their manicured gardens and huge cars they don't know how to drive live there. Still. I like trees. Something about their silence calms me. And I have a respect for them I don't have for much else.

I set up my gear, secure myself to my safety harness, and scale the trunk while the lady of the house hovers on a front porch that's bigger than the single room I call home.

"Are you sure you should be up there? The other chap was just going to cut it down."

I roll my eyes, tempted to pretend I haven't heard her, but I've learnt the hard way that ignoring certain conversations only extends them. I scan the area of the tree concerning me and then skin down, returning to earth. "I'm going to cut it down too, but not until I've trimmed the diseased sections. Otherwise I'll be sawing through the base with the risk of those weak branches landing on my head. Or yours."

The woman blinks. "Oh. Okay. Your colleague didn't mention

any of that."

Because he's an absolute melt. But I don't say it. I don't say anything. Just dead-eye the woman until she retreats into her palatial home without offering me so much as a cuppa. Bernard's most affluent customers are the worst hosts.

I turn my back on the house and gather what I need to trim the tree before I bring it down, then I climb again. At the top of the tree, I don't resist the urge to look out over the town. Never can. Being so separate from the world is the sole reason I never piss Bernard off enough to sack me. I live alone, work alone, and when I'm sitting with the birds, it's as though no other fucker exists.

Solitude.

Tranquillity.

It's a crying shame to shatter the vibe with a chainsaw, but that's life—my life, at least—and the white noise of the saw brings a detachment of its own.

I work through the diseased branches. Some are so fragile I break them with my hands. When I'm done with the south side of the tree, I shut the saw off and lean back to assess my progress. There isn't much to do on the other side, and it's already wobbly from the botched attempt to fell it that morning. *Half an hour and I'm gone.* I don't keep many promises, but the pub is calling my name.

Out of habit I glance over the horizon to the village green. The Red Lion turned their Christmas lights on last week, so it's easy to spot. I can almost taste the cold Guinness sliding down my throat, smell the wood fire, and hear the beeps and dings of my favourite fruit machine. Just a few more cuts—

The roar of a diesel engine blasts through my thoughts. Irritated, I spin around, searching for the source.

Headlights break through the fading daylight. A gritting lorry appears at the top of the slope, sliding on the icy tarmac. *Too fast. It's going too fast.* But the rest of the world seems to move in slow motion. I scramble to descend the tree trunk as the truck careens towards me and obliterates the fence in front of the big house. It hits the tree a split second later.

Falling lasts a lifetime.

TWO

Ludo

I bang my head against the bed rail just to hear something other than my own tripping brain. It's late, close to midnight, and the strangling silence of the sleeping hospital ward makes me want to throw things around and scream. Anything to disrupt the oppressive quiet.

Restless, I sit up. Lie down. Sit up again. Unwelcome energy buzzes in my veins, and a tremor shakes the hand that isn't encased in plaster. The effects of the general anaesthetic have long faded, and even the discomfort of having fresh metal pins inserted into my forever-damaged wrist isn't enough to quell the anxiety flaring in my gut.

I need to get out of here.

But escape isn't an option. The nursing team have been forewarned that I pose a flight risk and check my every move. I can barely use the bathroom without an escort, and the unwanted attention is almost as bad as the phantom ants crawling over my skin.

I lie down again, chest rising and falling too fast, and focus on the throbbing beneath the cast, the tugging sting of the stitches holding my skin together. It works for a while. Then I picture ants for real, imagine creepy bugs invading the space between my flesh and the plaster, and new agitation surges. Fresh sweat sticks my thin T-shirt to my back and the reverb in my brain hurts my ears. *I need . . . something.*

There's a handful of mobile screens on the ward. At home, my predilection for paranoia means I rarely watch TV, but trapped in hell, I'm desperate for distraction. *Maybe I can watch the weather on mute.*

I find a free trolley and wheel it closer to my bed, straining the only limb I possess that isn't a victim to the noise in my head. A nurse catches me, but it's the one who likes me—as much as she likes anyone. She helps position the TV and retrieves the remote.

"Quiet now," she says. "They're bringing someone down from intensive care, so you need to stay put, okay? No more wanderings tonight."

I've spent my entire adult life being spoken to like a child. I nod and lie down, curling up under the thin, grey blanket and scratchy sheet, fixing my gaze on the TV screen. The Weather Channel comes up trumps, and I lose myself in the moving screen of sleet and snow expected over the next few days. It excites me. I like the cold—the wind in my face, ice against my bare feet. It's so much more bearable than suffocating heat.

I close my eyes, willing sleep to carry me through until my morning lithium dose. The hospital fucked it up yesterday and today, feeding me half the dosage of my usual pill. *"Don't worry. You won't feel any different."* But they were wrong. Obviously. I feel different every day.

By the nurse station, the double doors swing open. Metal wheels scrape the rubber floor, and a bed carrying an unconscious man is pushed onto the ward.

I squint in the dim light. I drowsed through the handful of new faces that arrived immediately after my surgery, too out of it to take much notice, but as the bed passes, I've never felt more awake in my life. *Jesus.* Even bruised and bloodied, the man is *gorgeous.* And clearly under seventy; a rarity on this random overspill ward.

Orderlies push the bed to the high-dependency bays opposite

mine. A flurry of nurses work to hook the man up to machines while the ward sister and another man talk gravely at the foot of the bed. I'm enthralled but, as ever, so unsubtle it's painful. My friendly nurse meets my gaze, shakes her head, and draws the curtain around my bed, corralling the TV and me into our quiet corner.

But she leaves a gap, and as hard as I try, I can't look away.

The man has ink-dark hair, and what skin isn't hidden by wound dressings, blankets, and equipment is alabaster pale. The kind of skin that's so smooth to the touch you can never stop. *I wonder—*

Oh God. I swallow and shrink against my bed. *You absolute sicko. Look at the state of him.*

It's hard not to. With his leg plastered from foot to thigh and a crude tube contraption protruding from his ribcage, the man is a mess. A beautiful mess, but a mess nonetheless.

Word repetition, even unspoken, grates my nerves. I focus on the unconscious man and instantly regret it. The tube in his chest looks excruciating, and whatever misfortune has befallen him has happened recently enough for dried blood to still be smeared over his glorious skin.

I want to wipe it off.

But then, I also want the ground to swallow me whole, and I can't gauge which voice is loudest.

The second man to enter the ward is still deep in conversation with the ward sister. He's slimmer and older, but shares enough of the unconscious dude's dark good looks to be a relative. He scrubs a hand down his weary face. "Will he be okay?"

The sister nods and turns to leave. "We hope so."

What sort of answer is that? I frown and wonder why it matters to me, but the reedy man doesn't seem convinced either. He stops my nurse and repeats the question. I brace myself. I've only been on the ward a few days, but I know this nurse well enough to anticipate her brutal candour.

"Your cousin fell twenty feet, hitting a van, and then landed on concrete," she says. "He had a chest tube inserted in the field while he was trapped, and his leg is broken in three places. I imagine he won't be *okay* for quite some time."

She speaks with compassion, but her words hit the man as though she's slapped him. He takes a deep, shuddering breath and sinks onto a nearby chair while I bite my lip, abruptly and acutely aware that perhaps listening in is the ultimate disrespect to these strangers in the night. I glance around for something else to occupy my racing mind, but the TV no longer holds up.

A frantic desire to be somewhere else hits me, fast becoming all-consuming. My mind jumps, my heart pounds, and I'm crawling out of my own skin. If I could peel myself like an old satsuma and throw it away, I would. There aren't many parts of myself I wouldn't give up for the peace of mind I so often lack.

I press the call button. A new face appears. I grab my notes from the side of the bed and hold them out.

"Can I have a sleeping pill, please?"

Aidan

Beep. Beep. Beep.

I'm going to kill someone if it doesn't stop. Careful to keep my body still, I cast an irritated glare at the monitor taking up space at my bedside. It has the added attraction of letting me know I'm still alive, but that's about it. At this point, I'd happily die rather than hear another sound from it.

Drama queen.

Maybe, but combined with the insane amount of pain coursing through me, checking out seems a viable option.

Or chucking up.

Fuck. I swallow hard, trying to dispel the violent nausea swelling in my scratchy throat. Panic takes hold as I realise vomiting will involve movement, and a desperate, inhuman groan escapes me.

Pain.

"I know, mate. Use your morphine pump."

The voice is far away and nothing like any of the voices that have followed me into hell, but the mention of a morphine pump rings a distant bell. *You fell, remember? You broke your leg and had a tube shoved between your ribs.*

More nausea. I have zero clue where the mythical morphine pump has gone, but I know one thing for certain: I'm going to be sick, and it's going to hurt like a motherfucker.

That's two things, arsehole—

The devil on my shoulder is no match for my years-old reaction to extreme pain. Bile surges in my throat and my stomach contracts, triggering fiercer waves of agony. I lurched sideways and throw up into the darkness as another ragged sound tears from me. *I can't breathe. I—*

A cool hand touches my face, turning it gently. "There's an emesis basin right there, and I've put your pump by your left hand. It was on the floor."

"Ludo, back to bed, please."

The second voice is stern and one I recognise from the last time I upchucked on myself, but it's little comfort to me as the soothing palm slips from my cheek. For the brief moment it touched my skin, it grounded me. Without it, I'm swimming again, with nothing to cling onto but pain.

Sometime later, I open my eyes. A stark hospital ceiling, itchy sheets, and cold draughts greet me, but the burning in my chest has faded, and my leg is so numb it seems no longer attached to my body.

I shift cautiously to ease the stiffness from my shoulders and brave a glance around, but there's not much to see. The bed beside me is empty, and across the aisle, everyone seems to be asleep, if the hunched shape in the bed directly opposite is even a person.

Giving a shit is exhausting. I drop my head and consider passing out again, but before the thought completes, a tall figure darkens the end of my bed. A doctor who looks like he belongs on the set of an American hospital drama.

"Hello," he says. "I'm Dr Ramsey. Are you feeling awake enough to talk?"

I contemplate holding an actual conversation, something I avoid even when I'm not skewered on a hospital bed. Despite Dr Hotness, it doesn't hold much appeal. On the other hand, the desire to escape is strong, and the doctor likely knows more about when that might happen than the nurses I've cursed at and puked on. "I'm okay."

Dr Ramsey draws the curtain around the bed, pulls up a stool, and sits down. "Good. I know you've been quite sick overnight, so I've left you alone, but I want to get that chest tube out of you before I go home. It must be uncomfortable."

"It's not fun."

"I'll bet. You were a trooper when it went in, if it's any consolation. Didn't make a sound."

"Huh?"

"I was on the HELIMED team that extracted you from the accident site." Dr Ramsey makes a note on the clipboard he's holding. "I don't expect you to remember much of that though."

I'm having a hard time recalling what day it is, let alone the shit show my life has descended into while people have shoved tubes into every orifice. I remember the tree, the truck, and falling. After that, it's a blur of pain and confusion. "I don't remember you."

"I'll take that as a compliment. Hopefully the drugs worked and you didn't feel much."

"Uh-huh. Can I go home?"

Dr Ramsey shakes his head. "You're going to be with us for a while, I'm afraid. That chest tube needs to come out, and then the surgeons need to look at your leg again. We did what we could downstairs, but you'll likely need some rods inserted to help the bones reset."

"Surgery?"

"Yes."

"What else is wrong with me?"

"What are your other injuries?"

I nod. "I know I broke my leg . . . I felt it, but I don't know what happened to the rest of me."

Dr Ramsey sets his clipboard down and fixes me with a gaze that's somehow kind and intense at the same time. "Well, you fell pretty far. I think the tree you were working on was around thirty feet tall, but the van roof broke your fall a little."

"Super."

"Yes, I thought so. If you'd hit concrete from that height, we wouldn't be having this conversation."

I've got nothing. Literally nothing.

Dr Ramsey gives me a moment, then continues. "Okay, so your lung collapsed on impact, so we inserted a chest tube to expand it, and then I worked to free your leg from the tree while my colleague patched your head wound and kept you breathing. You gave us a bit of a scare on the chopper, but you're young and fit, so your lung held up. I'm confident you'll recover fully from that injury."

That injury. The ominous throb in my leg reignites, settling deep into my shattered bones. "What about my leg?"

The doctor's gaze flickers with something I can't decipher. "It's hard to say. The damage to the knee is severe. It will take some time to ascertain the best route for repair, and it's unlikely it'll ever be quite the same."

"But I'll be able to walk?"

"Yes. Perhaps even go back to work, but you need to be prepared to make changes. Adapting is how we survive, and you *did* survive a fall that should've killed you. Try to remember that when recovery kicks you in the tits."

I blink, unprepared for the good doctor's bluntness. It's so unlike anything I've ever heard from a health professional that I have no sensible response.

Clearly taking my silence as a sign the conversation is over, Dr Ramsey stands and plucks latex gloves from the dispenser on the wall. "Right then. Let's get rid of this tube."

THREE

Ludo

His name is Aidan. All the nurses call him Mr Drummond, but I saw his name on his chart when I retrieved his morphine pump from the floor.

That was yesterday. His face, twisted in such terrible pain, has haunted me ever since. From time to time, I hear his ragged groans. They're loudest when I'm asleep, and match the wretchedness in my soul so absolutely, I wake surprised to find my own leg is whole.

"Ludo?"

I tear my gaze from the curtains drawn around Aidan Drummond's bed and scowl at the *two* doctors who have woken me up—the surgeon who operated on my arm and the psychiatrist from the clinic attached to the hospital. "Hmm?"

"You have a slight infection," the surgeon says. "Nothing too major, but as you're without a spleen, I'd like to keep you in until it clears. Dr Farsi is going to update your lithium prescription so we don't get that wrong again, and I'm going to order some IV antibiotics for you."

"IV?"

"Yes."

"So I'll be stuck in bed?"

"We'll get you a pole," Dr Farsi interjects. "So you can use the bathroom and move around. I know you don't like to be confined."

Of course she does. Dr Farsi has been my psychiatrist for eighteen months, ever since the last incident that put me in hospital. There's little about the worst of me she doesn't know.

The surgeon pokes around at my plastered arm. "Sorry if it's a bit sore. I'm nearly done."

"It's fine," I say absently. "I like the pain."

I don't look at Dr Farsi again.

After extending my confinement to the ward, the doctors leave, walking close together. *They're either shagging or talking about you.* Paranoia licks my brain, but for once, the ghouls dancing through my consciousness aren't my primary concern. Another doctor exits the bay opposite. He seems familiar, though I can't say why, and I don't care. Doctors are doctors. After a while, they're all the same.

I return my attention to Aidan's bed. The departing doctor has left the curtain open and my breath catches. *He's awake.* It's the first time I've seen him not sleeping. Or so sick he can't open his eyes.

Sometimes my thoughts seem so loud I wonder if I've shouted them. This is one of those moments. Aidan shifts slightly, staring across the aisle in the kind of daze I miss when the sleeping pills wear off, leaving nothing but a metallic taste on my tongue.

I swallow to dislodge the sensation of something stuck in my throat. *They've poisoned you.* But as hard as I try to give a fuck, I just . . . don't. If they've poisoned me, I'll die, and death equals freedom. Right?

Wrong. You're okay, remember? You're safe. And you promised Rita you'd see her next week. No dying before then.

I swallow again and curl my hands into fists, chasing my thoughts one by one in an attempt to rationalise them. Some days it's easier than others, but being cooped up in hospital has triggered bad habits, and the temptation to run with my favourite catastrophic scenarios is strong.

"The fuck are you staring at?"

It takes me a moment to realise the question has come from the opposite bed and even longer to figure out it's directed at me. "What?"

"You're staring," Aidan repeats. "You want to piss off with that?"

I sit up, unmoved by the harshness lacing his morphine-heavy words. Irritation is an emotion I can deal with. Confrontation doesn't scare me if it's honest. "I'm thinking. Not staring. Are you okay?"

"What do you care?"

"Gives me something to do."

Aidan frowns. "Can you walk?"

"Um . . . yeah. Why?"

"Come closer. I can't hear you properly."

I glance at the nurses' station and slide carefully off my bed. My socked feet make no sound as I pad closer to Aidan's bed and slip behind the curtain. "Can you hear me now?"

"It was you."

"What was?"

"I was sick on you."

"Oh." Damn. I assumed he wouldn't remember that; he seemed so far gone. "Actually, you weren't sick on me. I got the bowl to you in time."

"Why?"

"Why what?"

"Why was it you?"

I shrug. "There was no one about and you'd lost your morphine pump. I figured you needed it . . . that's why you were moving around."

"I can't really remember."

"Fair enough." I start to back off, but Aidan holds his hand up to stop me.

"Come back," he says.

"Why?"

"Just do it, mate. Please?"

I shuffle back to his side, close enough for him to reach out and brush his fingers over the back of my hand.

"You're cold," he says. "And you're Ludo. I remember that."

His speech slows with each word, and his head lolls on the pillow, eyes drooping, distant and glazed.

I chuckle softly, surprising myself. "You don't seem like you'll remember anything at all next time you wake up."

"Nah, mate. I'll remember you."

Aidan

I'm still in hell. Caught between being in so much pain I'd rather eat my leg than endure it or being so stoned I have no clue where I am. The surgery is scheduled for a few days' time, and it can't come soon enough. Not that I'm expecting to get through it without a rerun of vomit-gate. Or being off my face on morphine.

You fucking pussy.

The food is shite too. I shove the plate of greasy chips away and rub a hand down my face. Then, as has become my habit over the last few days, I steal a glance at the bed opposite. Ludo is asleep, hooked up to an IV I can't remember being there the last time I checked in, which is generally every ten minutes when I'm awake.

Nonplussed, I look away. I can't figure out if my fascination with Ludo is boredom induced, a side effect of too much morphine, or linked to the lingering sensation of his cool palm against my cheek. Because *fuck*, there are a hundred gaps in my recent memories, but I can't get that shit out of my mind. Over and over I try to picture how the scene played out—me puking with Ludo trying to help me—but every image I conjure up makes me shudder in horror.

He saw me being sick.

For reasons I can't understand, it feels like the worst thing in the world.

I shift, trying to get comfortable. The incision in my ribcage is sore, but I can live with it. The pain in my leg, though . . . that shit is unreal. Coping with it takes up most of my time, and studying Ludo has become my favourite distraction. Especially when he's asleep and can't outstare me with his bottomless gaze.

The only other man I've ever watched sleep is my father. Weathered face, dirty hair. Reeking of whisky, cigarettes, and rage. By contrast, Ludo is angelic, his features boyish and smooth against dark hair tipped with white blond—a grown out bleach job. He's restless too, even as he sleeps, muttering and twitching. I wonder if he's dreaming . . . or stuck in a nightmare. Because that's the other thing about Ludo: wide and framed by thick lashes, his eyes are the most disturbed I've ever seen. I can't imagine him having pleasant dreams.

"Aidan?"

"What?" I glance up, unable to keep the habitual growl out of my voice.

The ward sister—the one with the good drugs—raises a brow. "Your cousin is here. It's not visiting hours for a while, but if you're quiet, I can sneak him in."

Michael. I suppress a sigh. Days have become a blur, and I have little idea how long I've been flat on my back, but Michael's appearance is inevitable. Of course it is. My life has gone to shit, and he *knows* how much I love an audience.

Not.

"Tell him to do one, will ya? I'm not in the mood to be lectured."

The sister twitches her eyebrow higher. "I can do that, but don't you think it would be nice to have some company for a while? It might take your mind off your discomfort."

"If that's what you think, then you don't know my cousin."

"I know him well enough to tell you he's been here every day since you were brought in. That must count for something."

I prefer the nurses who don't talk to me. It might be a coincidence, but they seem to have gentler hands too. Whatever. The sister is still frowning, lips pursed, hands on her hips.

She ain't going nowhere, boy.

Wow. I flinch. It's been a long time since I last heard my father's voice in my head. *These drugs are messed up.* "Fuck it. I don't care."

"Then I'll show him in."

"Super."

Five minutes later Michael stands at the end of my bed, an older, slimmer version of me in looks only—he's a much nicer person. "Hey. How are you doing?"

I roll my eyes. Regret it. "Fucking marvellous, mate. How are you?"

A ghost of a smile threatens his earnest expression. "You haven't lost your sense of humour then."

"Never had one."

"If you say so." Michael ventures closer and hovers by the chair the hot doctor sat in. "When is your surgery scheduled?"

"How do you know about that?"

"I spoke with your doctor a few days ago. I'm your next of kin, Aidan, and you've been out of it for days."

Days. Huh. I peer over Michael's shoulder. Maybe that explains my newfound obsession with the stranger across the aisle.

"Aidan?"

"*What*?"

Michael sighs. "Look, we need to talk about what's going to happen when you get out of here. The doctor told me you could be on crutches for months, and that's banking on you only needing one operation."

"What difference does any of that make to you?"

"A hell of a lot if you're going to need a place to stay and people to look after you. We're happy to have you live with us for a while, but it's going to take some shifting around."

I force myself to focus entirely on Michael and the fuckwittery spilling from his mouth. "Have you lost your bloody mind? I'm not moving in with you."

"Aidan, you have to—"

"I don't have to do anything. I've got a place of my own. Shitty ground floor bedsit, remember? I can live there even if they cut the damn leg off."

"Oh yeah? And what if you fall or need something you can't reach? Who's going to be there for you?"

"No one, but I'm used to that, eh?"

"That's not fair."

Of course it's not fair. Michael lives thirty miles away with a young family to care for. I'm not his responsibility. Never have been. And yet here we are. Again. Me in the shit and Michael believing it's on him to fix everything.

I dig deep for my least unpleasant facial expression. "Look, I appreciate the offer, but it's not necessary. I'll be fine in my place, and if I'm not, we can have this conversation all over again, okay?"

"It's not okay, Aidan. None of this is. You know the truck driver who hit you failed the breath test? The idiot was out-of-his-mind drunk."

"Lucky him."

"You're not angry?"

"I'm not anything, mate. I'm stuck in this bed for the foreseeable, and all I want to do is get some decent kip. You think you can help me with that by fucking off?"

"You're an arsehole."

"Yup."

Michael leaves. I listen to his footsteps fade and knock my fist on my temple, *hard*. It doesn't hurt as much as I need it to, and for once the fire in my leg is manageable enough for me to think clearly.

I don't want to think.

I reach for my morphine pump, but it's empty.

"You've used it all."

I open my eyes. Ludo's voice sounds so close I half expect to see him where Michael stood, but he's sitting on his own bed, cross-legged, cradling his injured arm against his chest. His hair is mussed and his eyes hooded. He doesn't look like he's been awake long. "Used all what?"

"The morphine. It clicks when it's empty and you have to wait until the next dose is due."

I know that. That damn-fucking click haunts me at night when I really do have nothing to think about except the agony searing every nerve. But somehow hearing Ludo say it makes it more frightening.

He breaks our stare off and goes back to flicking the cast around his wrist. I ponder what's wrong with him, then why I give a shit. *I don't give a shit.* But curiosity is a wicked thing. Add in boredom and pain and I'm apparently a brand new person. "What happened to your arm?"

Ludo raises his gaze, eyes still bleary and swollen. "Nothing recently. I smashed it up last year and it needed new pins."

"They're putting pins in my leg."

"I know. Your visitor has a loud voice."

"Michael? Seriously? I don't think that dude has ever shouted in his life."

"Maybe I was listening too hard then."

Ludo speaks without inflection, as though we have conversations like this all the time. As though it's normal for him to be listening and absorbing information *I* haven't paid enough attention to. Arsehole me wants to bite his head off. Tell him to mind his fucking business. But . . .

I'm so tired. And talking to Ludo seems to require every sense even without growling at him. Not that I've ever possessed much sense. "Are you bored?"

"Hmm?" Ludo is still flicking his cast. "Bored? With what? Being stuck in here? Or talking to you?"

"Either. Both."

Ludo laughs, and for a fleeting moment, I'm so captivated I'm scared our entire exchange has been a dream. But it's not a dream. He's real. And somehow I'm laughing too.

"I'm not bored with talking to you," Ludo says. "But I'm definitely bored on this ward. Until you, there's been no one to talk to at all."

"Is that a bad thing?"

"Yes. If I don't talk to other people, I talk to myself, and that never ends well."

His smile fades so I can't tell if he's joking. And I can't imagine that hearing his voice on a permanent basis could be much of an affliction. He has a rough London accent that's nothing like the stuck-up tones most knobheads in Buckbourne speak with. It reminds me of the cockneys on *Peaky Blinders*. "You can talk to me, mate. Can't promise I'll talk back though."

"Not a fan of your own voice?"

"Who is?"

"Point taken."

I'm still really fucking tired. I close my eyes, just for a second, praying Ludo will still be looking at me when I open them again, but the sound of metal on rubber brings me back to life. I open my eyes and he's shuffling towards my bed, his IV stand trailing behind him. My weary heart leaps, and confusion hits me in waves. I've never wanted someone to come and talk to me so much in my entire life, and I don't know what the fuck is happening to me.

My broken leg makes sense. This doesn't.

Ludo makes it to the chair by my bed and sits. He puts his hand on my arm. "I'm not cold anymore."

He isn't. In fact, he's blazing hot. "What's the matter with you?"

"I have an infection where they cut me. That's why I'm still here."

The thought of him not being here makes me feel sick. "Oh. Is that what the IV is for?"

"Yeah. Antibiotics. I don't like them, though." He points to a mess of plasters in the crease of his elbow. "That's why I keep taking the cannula out, but I can't go home until I'm better, so I need to stop doing that."

"Why don't you like the antibiotics if they're making you better?"

"I feel like I have snakes in my veins," he says as though it makes perfect sense.

Perhaps it does. With his hand still on my arm, I can't tell.

An odd urge to cover his hand with my own sweeps over me. I glance at him, hoping to dispel it before I make a tit out of myself, but my gaze falls on a scar on Ludo's face, and I'm knee-deep in a new rabbit hole. The scar runs along his jaw, half hidden by the scruff on his face, but it's ragged and angry, and I can't look at it for long without imagining how my leg will look when I finally get out of here. "How long will the antibiotics take to work? If you don't pull the cannula out, I mean."

Ludo shrugs. "I don't know. Maybe they told me and I wasn't listening."

"But you hear all my business?"

He treats me to a sheepish grin. "Sorry. You like your privacy."

It's not a question, but I nod anyway. "Don't you?"

"Sometimes. But too much of it is bad for my brain."

"Because you don't like your voice?"

"Exactly."

We reach an understanding I can't quite see, and his hand slips from my arm. My gaze darts to it, and I'm surprised to see he's left no mark. In my head, the heat from his touch is scorching, still burning strong, even now it's over.

"Are you worried about your operation?"

Slowly, I shake my head. "I don't think they could make it hurt any more than it already does."

"Did your chest tube hurt?"

"Hmm?"

Ludo leans closer, his wide eyes owlish. "The tube they put in your chest. I've never had one of those."

"You want one?"

"No." Something wicked dances in Ludo's expression. "I've broken lots of bones, though, and they took my spleen last time."

"Last time what?"

"Last time I fell."

I stare. Again. "How often do you fall?"

"For real or metaphorically?"

"I don't know what that means."

Ludo sighs and ruffles his already messy hair. "Neither do I."

FOUR

Ludo

His favourite colour is green. I don't want to tell Aidan that *my* favourite colour terrifies me, so I don't. Instead, I sit by his bed and we talk about music and the food we're going to eat when we go home.

He likes indie music, and he's craving a roast dinner. He's amused by my admissions. "You don't look like the classical music type."

"Who does?"

"Dunno. But I kind of expected you'd like grime and shit, with your London speak and all that."

I can't place his accent. It's definitely local, but mildly so, as though at some point he's been displaced from his roots long enough for them to fade. "I don't like grime music. And I got into classical when I was a kid. My cousin was a ballet dancer and I spent a lot of time watching him practice."

"She sounds more interesting than my cousin."

"Who does?"

"Your cousin."

"My cousin is a boy . . . well, a man now, I guess. I haven't seen him for a long time."

Aidan grunts. "You can have mine."

"The skinny bloke who's always here?"

"Always?"

"Uh-huh. I've seen him every day since you got here."

Something flashes in Aidan's eyes. It's so fleeting I wonder if I've imagined it. But for once, I trust myself. Or maybe it's more that Aidan's expression is usually so painfully blank.

"He won't come anymore," he says after a protracted silence. "I think he just wanted to check I wasn't fucked up enough to be his problem."

"In what way?"

Aidan gestures at himself, from the plaster encasing his leg, to the butterfly stitches in his temple. "Apparently I might not be able to look after myself when they let me go home. Which makes it his job, according to him."

"What do you think?"

He shrugs. "I think it doesn't matter what state I'm in when I get out of here; I'm going home, and I'll be fine on my own, because I always am."

I'm missing a lifetime of ways to understand him. I want to tell him that it's okay to let people help him, but I don't. Because maybe it's not. Maybe being self-sufficient is how he survives and I can learn something from him.

I touch his arm again. "Yeah. You're gonna be fine."

Aidan

Ludo comes to talk to me every day, twice, sometimes, if he's up to it.

I can't figure out if he's okay . . . if he's getting better. When he touches me, his skin still blazes, and one day I wake up to see that it's him being sick over the side of his bed instead of me. When it's over, he looks at me and smiles, and something tells me that his physical ailments barely scratch the surface.

But I don't get the chance to ask him more questions. An orderly comes to take me for an X-ray, and when I get back, something has changed. The ward smells intensely of the disinfectant fluid the cleaning staff smear over the floors on a daily basis, which is a welcome change from the "lunch" cooking somewhere in the hospital. But it's not that—it's Ludo. Something has changed with *him*. A different IV is hooked up to him, and an oxygen mask covers his face. He has a visitor too, a kindly looking woman who's reading a book as he sleeps.

I wonder if it's his mum, and something sharp scrapes my insides. I loved my mum, even though I've spent my entire life angry with her for dying.

The orderly manoeuvres my bed into its parking spot. The space is less cluttered now the big machines have been moved. All that's left is an IV stand, and a nurse comes to reconnect me. *Don't ask. Don't ask. Don't ask.* "What's wrong with Ludo?"

Damn it.

The nurse shoots me a curious glance. "He's a bit poorly today."

"What's wrong with him?"

"I can't tell you that, sweetheart. Maybe you can ask him later, when he feels better."

The assumption that he *will* feel better should comfort me. It doesn't. "Is that his mum?"

"No."

She doesn't elaborate, but something about her one-word answer prickles my skin. Until today, Ludo's had even less visitors than me, giving him a grand total of zero. If the woman isn't his mother or a relative, then who the hell is she?

Staring brings me no closer to finding out, so I search for something else to do. But it's hard. I don't have any books, my phone is smashed to bits, and I've yet to figure out how to claim one of the ward's mobile TVs.

You could always, like, ask. But I know I won't. It's a Drummond thing to suffer in silence. Besides, watching TV at home sends me to sleep, and I don't want to sleep right now. I want to watch over Ludo to make sure he's okay and ignore the fact that I never cared if *anyone* was okay before I met him.

"Mr Drummond?"

I startle awake. Despite my best intentions, I've dozed off and somehow slept through my bed being moved to a different spot on the ward. "What the fuck?"

The nurse treats me to a steely glare before her expression softens. "We needed your high-dependency bay back, so we've moved you down here."

I blink rapidly. "Who did you need it for? Someone new?"

She doesn't answer. Just hands me a cardboard cup of pills.

I swallow them and drink the water she hands me. My legs hurt—that's right, both of them, because it isn't enough that one is broken, the other is protesting at being unused for so long. Muscle pain, spasms, throbbing joints. Fuck my whole goddamn life.

The nurse wanders off, leaving me to take stock of my new surroundings, not that I can see much of them. I'm in a dead end, so there's a wall on one side of my bed and the curtain is drawn around the other. The bed opposite is occupied, but it's not Ludo. It's an old man eating yoghurt with a pen lid, and I wonder if I've been dropped onto another fucking planet.

It doesn't help that the problem of having nothing to do remains. Being alone with my thoughts has never been an issue before; I generally don't have any beyond my next wage packet, but the good drugs have done weird things to me. Suddenly I'm fretting over the food in my freezer that will spoil when the electricity tokens run out and hoping someone feeds the manky stray cat who's always trying to kip on my couch. And I'm worrying about Ludo. What if the critical care bed was for him? He had an infection last time we spoke, and it wasn't getting better. What if he has sepsis? Or one of those flesh-eating hospital bugs I've seen splashed across the tabloids Bernard hoards in his van?

My heart turns over despite logic reasoning that my bed could've been given to anyone. After all, if Ludo needed my bed and I was well enough to take his, surely they'd have simply swapped us.

Logic has always been my friend, apathy too, and common sense. But all three are lacking as my mind turns over a dozen scenarios that could've brought me to this moment. My brain hurts. I touch the gash on my temple and wonder if I hit it harder than the docs are telling me. If something unseen is broken and that's why I can't get Ludo out of my thoughts. Head injuries change personalities, right?

Yeah, but you're still a prick.

Valid. I prove it to myself by ignoring the old gent across the aisle when he tries to talk to me and being obnoxious to the fella who brings my dinner.

And I don't eat. Ludo warned me not to rinse my morphine pump on an empty stomach, but I do it anyway, because he's not here, and I don't want to think about how reliant I've become on his company. On three days of random conversations with a stranger. Or maybe it's the sum total of six times he's touched me. Fingers brushing mine, a light thumbstroke on my forearm, and his soothing palm cupping my cheek. He only did that once, and I'm still half-convinced I dreamed it, but I'm not dreaming now. I'm living a nightmare. The only light in this dark fucking cavern is him.

And he isn't here.

Somehow I sleep some more, and I wake to silence sometime later. Significant time has passed, though I have no clue how much. A day. A week. Who gives a fuck?

I rub my face. For however long I've been here, I've convinced myself that my surroundings haven't mattered, that if I can only get the hell out of here, everything will be okay, but as I take in the unfamiliar bed bay with its broken cabinet and a chair that's the wrong colour, it *does* matter. My bed, though it's the same one I've been stuck in for who-the-hell-knows how long, feels like a raft adrift, and a desperate need to escape overwhelms me.

Heart in my mouth, I sit up, searching for something—anything

—I can use as makeshift crutches. I need fresh air. I need to go home. *Michael wants to help . . . he can pick me up.*

Being upright makes me dizzy. I brace myself on the side of the bed and suck in deep breaths that go nowhere. My good leg tingles as though it anticipates the excitement of my ridiculous plan. I ease it off the bed, finally grateful for the thick sock covering my uninjured foot. *Now what?*

For all my enthusiasm, I have no idea. My arms are strong enough to hold me up, but everything I can see to aid me has wheels. *Fuck it.* Maybe I'll just slide on my arse until I fall into a lift shaft or some shit. It's not like my life could get any worse right now.

"What are you doing?"

I jump a fucking mile. Someone is behind me, and I realise in my eagerness to be the stupidest man alive that I'm facing the wrong way. That any attempt to move forwards will take me straight into a fucking brick wall.

The irony is biblical and so devastating that I fail to register who the bemused voice belongs to until shuffling footsteps round my bed and Ludo stands in front of me.

He's all dark brows and the beginnings of a wicked grin. "Well you've fucked that up, haven't you?"

FIVE

Ludo

Aidan looks how I feel—tired, fragile, and frightened of something he doesn't understand. He's also in a mess, half out of bed, one foot hovering over the floor, frowning as though he doesn't remember how he got there.

I'm no use to anyone, never have been, but something drives me to take his arm and ease him back onto his bed. "You look like you're trying to escape."

"I am." But Aidan lets me manoeuvre him until he doesn't have the appearance of a desperate man on the edge of a cliff. "Whoa, you're strong."

"Why does that surprise you?"

"Because you've only got one working arm and you're skinny as fuck."

He has a point, but it's not one I'm prepared to concede. Being freakishly strong, despite a lack of timber, runs in my family. Ask my cousin Angelo, and tell him I said hi. You might have to remind him who I am, but hey. No conversation is ever wasted.

Aidan is staring at me, and I realise I've done that thing—the one where I get lost in a bitterness that drowns me if I let it. Most days I have bigger problems than the fact that my family have forgotten me, but others it sneaks up on me and I can't help listening to the meanest of many voices in my head.

You aren't even crazy enough for them to remember.

Aidan clicks his fingers in front of my face. "The fuck did you go?"

I blink. "What?"

"Never mind."

He drops his hand, his gaze too, and I feel totally exposed. The panic that drove me from my bed to seek him out returns and a strangled sound escapes me. I thought he was dead, for no other reason than I came out of my infection-induced haze to find him gone. A rational person would've figured he was moved to a lower dependency bed, but I'm not a rational person.

Aidan drops back on his pillow and winces as the jerky movement ricochets through him. "I can't handle this place."

"Cabin fever?"

"And then some. I'm gonna lose my mind if I don't see daylight soon."

"There's a window right there." I point to one two feet from his bed. "It's dark now though."

Aidan's gaze flickers to the window. "See? I hadn't even fucking noticed."

"Why would you when you have other things to worry about?"

"Because that *is* what I've been worried about."

I can't argue with his logic, and I worry that I'm keeping him up. It's the middle of the night and he should be sleeping, or resting if he's like me and finds the silent ward deafening. I step back. His hooded eyes flare and he sits up again.

"Where are you going?"

"I don't know."

"That doesn't make any sense."

"What does?"

Aidan has no answer to that. I claim a point back, and the implication that he wants me to stay makes me feel . . . alive, I guess. After a quick glance at the deserted nurse station, I sit on the chair at his bedside. "When did they move you here?"

"Yesterday, maybe? Or maybe it was today. I've lost track."

"Me too."

"I'll bet. You've been asleep for days."

"Have I?"

He nods. "I thought they were giving you my bed when they moved me. It freaked me out."

"Why?"

Aidan starts to speak and then stops. His hands are apparently fascinating to him. He turns them over, examining them. He has scarred knuckles, as though he fights a lot or has a manual job. Yeah. He definitely has a manual job. There's no way this dude sits in an office all day.

"Are you a thinker?" he asks suddenly.

The question catches me off guard. "What does that even mean?"

He shrugs. "You seem to forget we're talking sometimes."

"Not on purpose."

"Didn't say it was."

His childish response suits me. It shouldn't, but it does, and the draw to him intensifies enough for me to slide the chair closer to the bed. "I'm tired."

"Me too," he says. "So why aren't we asleep?"

I consider what I've asked myself so many times and give him the only answer I've ever found. "Because we're uncomfortable in our own skin, but that might be temporary for you."

"But it isn't for you."

This time it's not a question, but I nod anyway. "I'm a little messed up."

He doesn't answer for a moment, but he's conquered his sudden fascination with his hands, oblivious to the fact that he's sparked another obsession in me—that I can't stop documenting his scars and committing them to my contrary memory.

"Are you feeling better?" he asks.

"Better from what?"

"Your infection. You were really sick."

I start to cringe, and then I remember that he's been sick too, and whatever he saw doesn't seem to matter so much. "I feel better, but I'm not sure I like that. Being under the weather killed some time."

I've never met anyone who understands statements like that, but Aidan nods. "Valid. Is the infection better, though?"

"A bit. They say it will take another five days to completely go."

"How do you feel about that?"

I can think of no logical reason for him to ask me that question, but as I shoot him a quizzical glance, it clicks. He's asking about my problems to deflect and distract from his own, and damn, if I don't get that. "I meant what I said about being sick filling some time, but I don't like having an infection. It makes me feel like I've got invaders under my skin, and the longer I have it, the longer I'm stuck here."

"You want to go home," he states.

"Yes, just like you." Though I'm fairly sure that's our only similarity. Despite what he says, Aidan is far stronger than me—*big* and strong, with working hands, and the healthy skin of a man who spends most of his time outside. Not like me. Living alone scares the shit out of me, but perversely I can spend weeks at a time indoors. It's as though my brain wants me to feel as terrible as possible, and only then will it leave me alone.

Aidan hums. It's a deep, rumbling sound that comes from somewhere I want to be. "Who was the woman who came to see you?"

"What woman?"

His resting bitch face deepens to an actual frown. "You had a visitor, a woman . . . at least, I think you did. This morphine shit is sending me crackers."

"Some of us are already there."

"I want to be your friend." Aidan clamps his mouth shut, as if his words have surprised him as much as they have me.

I let it slide. Perhaps it *is* the morphine, or Stockholm syndrome. Whatever. It's what we both need and I'll call him mate all night long if it helps him feel better. "If the woman exists, then I don't know who she is, which tells me she was probably a volunteer from the mental health charity the NHS uses for crisis management."

"You didn't notice her sitting by your bed?"

That he doesn't so much as twitch at the mention of mental health warms me to him even more. "Maybe not. I don't remember much of the last few days."

"Because of the infection?"

"Yeah, and the sedative they gave me to compensate for the fact I'd puked all my lithium up."

Experience told me there were other reasons to sedate me, but if I cling to every single waver in my mental health, it will become all I am, if it hasn't already.

Aidan's gaze is drilling a hole in the side of my head. I force myself to look at him, to accept his curious stare, and tell him the truth. "I have bipolar disorder," I say, "among other things."

"What other things?"

"Anxiety, paranoia, depression. Sometimes it's symptomatic of the disease; sometimes, it's just . . . me."

"Bipolar." Aidan says it as if he's turning it over in his head and matching it to somewhere he's heard it before.

I sigh. "Whatever you're thinking, don't. I have *real* bipolar, not the trendy one where you go to a clinic and come out with bigger boobs."

"You want bigger boobs?"

I laugh, and lights come on, both in my soul and somewhere on the darkened ward. "Not especially, but a week in this nut house has done strange things to me already, so who the hell knows. I'd better go."

"What?"

"I should go," I repeat. "Before they catch me and put me in restraints."

He can't tell if I'm joking, and I don't elaborate either way. I rise and he catches my hand in his, just for a moment. The contact is fleeting and wonderful, and I don't understand how I feel as he lets go. Or why he did it.

"You'll come back, won't you?" he whispers.

I nod as footsteps approach. "I'll come back tomorrow."

SIX

Aidan

When I was a kid, I spoke so rarely that my teachers thought there was something wrong with me. They sent me to a speech therapist who concluded I was a sullen little git who needed to get out more, so I joined the football club until I got kicked out for fighting.

I have no explanation for what's happening to me now. For how the few hours a day Ludo sits with me have become the highlight of my miserable life, and how much I *talk* when I run out of questions to ask him.

He wants to know about the trees I save instead of the ones I cut down, and he doesn't ask how I came to fall out of one.

"It depends why I'm working on it," I explain as he eats an orange, the only edible thing that came with lunch. "If the landowner wants it cut down and destroyed, there's not much I can do about it, but Bernard, my boss, charges less for treating diseased trees, so councils and nature trusts usually opt for that."

Ludo meticulously removes the pith from his orange segment before he slides it into his mouth. "How do you save a diseased tree?"

"Depends how sick it is."

"Uh-huh."

I take that as my cue to continue. "Like, if the tree is dying, sometimes it's kinder to remove it, to give up the resources you might use trying to save it to other trees."

"That makes sense."

"Yeah, but it takes a lot for a tree to be a lost cause. I never make the decision in one day. I always go back, unless someone else has already tried to fell it and I have to finish the job." I don't add that this particular habit has caused more run-ins with Bernard than anything else or that another tree surgeon's sloppy work is what has landed me flat on my back. I don't say anything like that, because the truth is, I'm trying not to think about it. Chances are, I'll never climb another tree, for fun or otherwise, and I'm not down with accepting that.

"What if a tree can be saved? What do you do?"

Ludo's soft voice brings me back to the present, and I'm so fucking grateful to him I nearly say so. Then I realise he's asked me the same question twice, and I haven't given him an answer. "Check the roots and surrounding area for anything that's limiting nutrition. Then I cut the diseased bits off, but you have to do it right. You can't just go at it with a saw and hope for the best."

"In case you end up worse than when you started?"

"Exactly. Trees are like humans. Open wounds don't do them no good."

Ludo chews slowly, deliberately, and drops the rest of his orange on my tray—he's already disposed of the weird meat dish neither of us could eat. Somehow he knew I couldn't look at it. Or maybe *he* couldn't look at it and the distinction between us is blurred.

I don't like the look in his face though. And I don't want him to go hungry. "Have my yoghurt."

"Huh?"

"My yoghurt." I push it towards him. "I've gone off them."

"Why?"

"Do I need a reason?"

Ludo shrugs and takes the yoghurt and I watch him eat it,

tracing every swallow as though I can track the calcium into his slender bones.

Why's that so important to you?

I have no idea about that either, and perhaps this is what my life will be from now on—a never-ending series of shit I don't understand. Before . . . this, before *him*, my existence was simple. I hated everyone and they didn't much like me, and I was okay with that. Worrying about other people never crossed my mind, and I shoved aside anyone who dared to care about me. Michael said it was as though I flicked a switch in my brain . . . like I did it on purpose.

Maybe I did.

A nurse exits the nurse station and begins her rounds of the beds, telling visitors they have to leave. Ludo sighs, and immediately my senses jump with a desperate need to find out why. I don't ask though. That would be simple. Instead I tilt my head sideways and hope he'll get the hint.

"I have a psychiatrist coming to see me today," he says. "She wants to change my medication."

"Why?"

He shrugs. "I may have had a mini meltdown over the last few days. I do that sometimes, when my brain can't decide if it wants to be yellow or black."

"Huh?"

Another sigh, and Ludo stands, still holding my yoghurt pot and a spoon. "Manic or depressed. Up or down. She doesn't listen when I tell her I'll be fine if they'd only let me go home."

I run my gaze up and down his slim legs . . . legs that are currently in a far better condition than my own. "You can't make a run for it?"

"Nah. They'll section me. Good idea, though. Ten years ago I might've got away with it."

He ducks around the curtain before I can respond, and a heavy weight settles over my chest, like it does every time he slips away. Some days he comes back for an evening visit, but I already know this isn't one of those days, and an irrational hatred for his psychiatrist spreads through me until it's all I can think about. I bring my hands to my face and drive my fists into my eye sockets. *You have no right to think anything about his psychiatrist. You don't know shit.*

But I want to. And that scares me. Out in the real world, I dip when I catch feelings for people, often after offending them to the point where they won't come looking for me. But I can't do that here, can't do it with Ludo, and the flip side of being desperate for his company has become an obsession.

A nurse brings me a dose of the codeine pills the docs have replaced my morphine pump with. I pretend to swallow them but stash them with my morning dose under my pillow. I'll take them tonight, when I'm sure Ludo won't come back, praying they'll keep me asleep until morning.

You daft prick. But I can't help it. The solitude that was once my BFF has started to suffocate me, and even if that doesn't kill me, the irony will.

Later that day it's my turn for an unwelcome welfare visit—a policeman who wants my accident statement.

"I don't have one. I was up, and then I was down."

The vague echo of Ludo's words bugs me enough to ignore the officer's resigned sigh. Perhaps he's found out I don't have the best history with coppers. Whatever. I don't care. I have nothing to say to him that doesn't involve being at the top of the world and then at the bottom.

Up and down.

Yellow and black.

Ludo

I'm beginning to hate Dr Farsi. When she screws with my normal, it's hard to remember the times when she's been the only constant in my life. That she's a *good* doctor, and it's me, as always, messing things up.

"I don't want to take more lithium. It fucks me up."

Dr Farsi slow blinks like she always does when I so very rarely swear at her, as though my colourful language is a validation for whatever she's itching to tell me about how I should feel. "Ludo," she says after years of addressing me with my whole name. "The dosage you're on may not be high enough, given the episodes you've had in the last week."

"Anxiety isn't bipolar. You've told me that a hundred times."

"Yes, but one can exacerbate the other. Controlling your bipolar effectively will make the rest of your life easier."

I scowl. "Not if it makes me a zombie. I'd rather feel everything than nothing."

It's a conversation that goes round in circles. Eventually I agree to the higher dose just to get rid of her, reasoning with my anxious self that I can cut the tablets in half. Or ditch them—

No. You don't do that anymore, remember?

Of course I remember. Mania and meds mess with my short-term memory, but I never forget nightmares. Can't, because they're real, and so when the little paper cups come around, I swallow the new pill.

Numbness creeps through me far quicker than it should. It's psychosomatic and I know it, but knowing something and believing it isn't the same thing. I picture the numbness as the army of ants I see every day, marching en masse to ambush my mood. I let them for a little while, but agitation overwhelms me. I have to move, even if I only get as far as the next bed before a nurse tells me to return to my own.

Luck is rarely on my side, but today the nurse doling out the drugs pays me no heed as I ghost past her. I go to the bathroom and brush my teeth while I stare at myself in the mirror, even though I know it will do me no good.

My skin is too pale. My English father robbed me of the chance to have my cousin's Mediterranean complexion. I lack Angelo's poise too. Always have. Where he was a beautiful child, all big brown eyes and grace, I was gangly and awkward, and now, though I've grown into my limbs, I'm sullen to those who don't know me and inexplicable to those who do.

Aidan falls somewhere in the middle.

It wasn't my intention to visit him again today. Some days I can't help myself. Others I fight to remember what happens when my brain becomes obsessed. When it can't let go of things that aren't mine. On those days, I visit him once and try not to imagine trailing my fingertip along his strong forearm like I did one time. I try not to imagine anything at all, to live in the moment and enjoy the bubble I've built around the short time I get to spend with him. Aidan isn't much of a conversationalist, but that's okay. Even his silence soothes me in ways I can't explain.

I'm close to his bed before I know it, but for the first time ever, he's not alone. A grave-faced doctor is sitting in *my* chair, and my heart turns over. Sometimes, when I force myself not to stare at Aidan too much, I forget he's hurt. The gash on his head has healed to an angry line, and a series of plain T-shirts now cover the bruises and scrapes from his fall. He's taken to hiding his leg under a blanket, as if he doesn't want to look at it, and I'm so hypnotised by the rest of him that I forget it's there.

Maybe my bad memory is convenient. Selective. Protective. I've given up any attempt to make sense of it. But there's one thing I know for sure—a doctor who frowns like that is bad news.

The doctor doesn't look like he's going anywhere, so I go searching for a TV instead. I find one on the far side of the ward, and the return trip puts me in sight of Aidan's bed again. He's alone now, and it's too easy to push the TV close enough to him that he glances up and spots me.

His lips twist into the closest he's ever come to an actual smile, though his eyes are tight with stress. "I didn't think you'd come back."

"Ever?"

"No. Today. Thought you might want some time to yourself after seeing your shrink."

Shrink. I've always hated that word. My twisted imagination has been known to convince me that it's what they're trying to do—to legit *shrink* my brain—and I cringe every time I hear it. But I don't cringe now. Aidan speaks simply. Perhaps it's time to listen simply too.

I focus on his actual words. "Nah. Shrink time is think time. I've had enough of that for one day."

"That bad?"

I wheel the TV closer, pushing it with my good arm so it trundles along like the ancient TV trolleys I remember from primary school, the ones with a VHS consoles no one could work. "It wasn't my favourite."

Aidan accepts my answer with a grunt and eyes the TV. "How did you get that? Do you have to pay for it?"

He's been here ten days . . . I think. How can he not know about the TV trolleys? I scan his bay for books and magazines or a set of weathered headphones like mine. But I find nothing and can't help but speculate what he's been doing all this time. Whenever I creep up on him, he's either asleep or staring at the ceiling. Is that seriously *all* he's been doing?

Damn. He'll be as batshit as me in no time.

I position the TV at the end of his bed and pull the curtain around it to let any pilferers know it's taken. "They're free," I say. "You just have to know where to nab them from."

"Oh. Well that's me fucked then. Don't think I'll be nabbing anything for a while."

"You can't use crutches? Not that they'll be much good if you're pushing a trolley."

Aidan sighs. "I could probably make do and hop along behind it . . . maybe, if they'd let me up, but I'm having surgery tomorrow, so I'm going to be flat on my back again for the foreseeable."

I somehow forgot about the doctor I saw loitering on my last visit. And that Aidan has been due to have surgery any day now. My heart turns over, and the pins in my wrist seem to throb. "Tomorrow?"

"Yeah. And my X-rays are messed up, so it's going to be a longer procedure than they thought."

"How long?"

"Four hours."

"Jesus—" I slap my hand over my mouth, for my benefit and his. However stoic my new friend is, he's got to be worried. "Sorry."

"It's okay." Aidan stretches out a muscular arm and beckons me closer. "That's pretty much my reaction too. How long did your operation take?"

"I don't know. They sedated me before the anaesthetic, so I lost track of time."

"What about after? Did it hurt?"

He's definitely worried. I consider bullshitting him to ease his fears, but I can't do it. Even with honourable intentions, dishonesty has never done me any good. "It hurt a lot at first. Use the morphine pump. If you've not had any for a few days, it should knock you out."

Aidan's gaze flickers, but the shadow is gone before I can decide if I've imagined it or not, and I realise that I'm hovering by the TV like a weirdo.

I venture ever closer to him and hand over the remote. "It's got Freeview. Just use the channel buttons to flick through."

"What were you going to watch?"

"Um . . ." Again, the urge to make something up is there. Again, I suppress it. "The weather. I can't really watch anything else."

I wait for him to ask why not, but he doesn't. He turns the TV on and jerks his head at the empty chair beside him. "I'm down with the weather."

He's humouring me. He has to be. But I sit anyway and help him find The Weather Channel. A storm is brewing, apparently, with gale-force winds and heavy rain. Aidan's habitual frown deepens and I can't help but touch his arm . . . with my fingertip, obviously. "What's wrong?"

"Hmm?"

"You're thinking hard enough to break something."

"In my brain?"

"Maybe." I try for a grin and hope it's convincing.

Aidan opens the cabinet on the other side of the bed and retrieves a yoghurt he's saved from dinner. He hands it to me with a shrug. "Storms mean damaged trees, which means work, lots of work that I'm missing out on while I'm stuck in here."

I peel the lid from the yoghurt pot and pry the plastic spoon from its hiding place. The yoghurt is fudge flavoured. At home when I'm fighting the urge to be manic or crawling out from under a vicious low, it's the only thing I can eat. "Are you worried about money?"

Aidan snaps his gaze from the TV. For a moment he seems cross, and then his face softens enough for me to dip the spoon into the yoghurt. "I *was* worried about money," he says, "until the surgeon came around. Now I'm so fucked there's no bloody point."

I retrace the few conversations we had about the tree surgeon work he clearly enjoys. He works for someone . . . but the name escapes me. "Will you lose your job?"

"Nah, Bernard likes me too much, but technically, I'm a subcontractor—if I don't work, I don't get paid, and I was already in the shit before this happened."

I tap my fingers on Aidan's bed rail. His tone is casual, but genuine worry lines his lovely face, marring his rugged good looks. "Your boss won't bung you a few quid?"

"Dunno."

"Have you asked him?"

"No."

"Maybe you should. You got hurt on the job; that's got to be bad for business, and for him, if he has a heart."

"Uh-huh."

He doesn't want to talk about this, so I take the snippet of information he's let fly and stash it away. I don't know much about much, but surviving, somehow, without the capacity to hold down a regular job is something I excel at.

For long minutes, Aidan watches The Weather Channel while I watch him and try to find the answer to his problem. My brain is a jumble of incomplete theories and aborted thoughts. Sifting through them takes time, and I'm *tired.* I slump in my chair. Aidan notices and lowers his bed rail. "Lean on the bed if you want. I mean, if it's more comfortable for you."

He knows . . . knows that leaning backwards sometimes makes me feel as though I'm falling, and I don't like it. I've never spent time with another person without having to explain my every nuance. Maybe with Aidan it's because he doesn't care, that he enjoys my company merely because without it he'd be alone twenty-four seven, but I make the executive decision that it doesn't matter and dump my arms on his bed.

I rest my head on my good arm and fight to keep thinking as I realise my face is a few centimetres from Aidan's bicep. He has amazing muscle tone, lean and strong, but still soft enough for me to wish my cheek could be pressed against his skin instead of my own. I close my eyes. My brain quiets to a dull roar and I'm almost asleep when a sharp voice drags me back to the real world.

"Ludo, get back to your own bed. Sorry, Mr Drummond. He does know not to bother the other patients."

"He's not bothering me," Aidan snaps as I raise my head. "Leave him alone."

The nurse glares. "He's not supposed—"

"To what? Talk to his friends? Piss off."

"Aidan—"

He silences me with a furious scowl and turns back to the nurse. "He's fine, honestly. I asked him to sit with me."

The nurse glances between us, clearly unconvinced, but whatever she sees in Aidan persuades her to back off.

She vanishes without another word, leaving me to stare at Aidan with my stomach in my throat. "You didn't have to do that. They're always chasing me back to my bed."

"Yeah well, they're not very good at it if they've never caught you with me before."

True. But I doubt it's occurred to anyone that Aidan would want to talk to me. He doesn't talk to anyone else. I've heard the nurses calling him Mr Moody, and after tonight I reckon he's probably cemented that.

He's not moody with me though. And he called me his friend, in a roundabout way, which makes me smile.

Aidan cocks his head sideways. "What're you grinning at?"

"Dunno. I'm loopy when I'm tired."

"You should probably go back to sleep then." He points at the exact spot my head was before and turns back to the TV as if it makes perfect sense.

Lacking any better ideas, I lay my head back down, and my eyes fall closed like weighted shutters. I *am* tired, and something—*everything*—about Aidan's silent company makes me feel safer than I have in a long time.

After a little while, he drapes his arm over my shoulders, solid warmth tying me down to the world.

It *doesn't* make perfect sense. It doesn't make sense at all.

But I like it.

SEVEN

Ludo

I wake too late to see Aidan again before he's taken away for his surgery. As I lie on my bed counting my heartbeats in the hope of slowing them down, I dimly remember a nurse hustling me away from him at some point in the night, but I don't recall what she said to me. How can I when all I can think of is Aidan's arm around me and whether he put it there on purpose?

I think he did. But then, I've thought things before and been horribly wrong.

Maybe it's best not to think.

At all.

Ever.

The morning drags on. I keep my anxiety at bay trying to figure out a solution to Aidan's income issues, but when I fail to come up with anything useful, the flood gates open, and before long I'm pacing around like a caged animal.

Dr Farsi brings me my increased lithium prescription along with a new anti-depressant she wants me to try. "Fewer side effects," she says. "But you can*not* suddenly stop taking it, Ludo. Call me if you feel like you might do something like that."

She knows me so well, but the finality to our exchange makes me wonder if I'll see her again before the surgeon boots me out, and new disquiet crackles in my already spiky brain. I've waited days for my magic pass out of here, but with Aidan in surgery, the thought of leaving *him* is so terrifying my legs stop working.

I stagger to my bed and crawl onto it. No one has even mentioned discharging me, but my consciousness is so conditioned to jump into catastrophes that haven't yet happened that I'm practically home already, hyperventilating on my lumpy old couch because I'll never know if some bloke I barely know has made it out of surgery okay.

My breath comes too fast, and though the fever that came with my infection has faded, I'm hot all over. I strip my baggy hoodie and toss it as far away from me as I can. Cool air hits my skin and I welcome the chill that spreads through my body, willing it to extinguish the smouldering, irrational nerves in my gut. *Think.* But I can't. Aidan has been gone for hours, and I've lost the ability to calculate if it's logical for my stomach-churning anxiety to mean anything.

Someone brings me lunch. When I was first admitted, the nurses would check I ate every meal, but they've grown complacent in recent days—actually, since Aidan got here—and no one sees me dump the contents of my tray into the bin.

I curl up on my bed again, a crazed mantra playing on a loop in my head. *He'll be okay. He'll be okay. He'll be okay.* But the thing about baseless fear is that after a while, the trigger ceases to matter. There's no connection to anything real. Just crippling terror. I jam my fist in my mouth and swallow a scream of frustration—at me, at *him.* It's not fair. I don't know Aidan. He doesn't know me. And nothing about our week-long friendship deserves this level of angst.

Nothing does.

It's mid-afternoon by the time I come full circle. Aidan still isn't back, but no one has come to discharge me either, and my favourite nurse has let slip that my surgeon isn't even here today.

My misguided red alert fades from razor sharp to a butter knife. As ever, I find it hard to reconcile with how dramatic my imagination can be. I've spent days at peak levels of anxiety . . . weeks. One time, I bit my nails so bad it took months to grow them back. Dr Farsi says anxiety is part of my bipolar, but I'm not always convinced. Today is neither yellow nor black, but a heady mix of colours that don't stay still long enough for me to decipher.

Dinner comes. I'm still not hungry, but I eat this time. I have to if I have any hope of not being a juddering wreck when Aidan comes back. When I'm done, I sit on the edge of my bed, breathing slowly, deliberately, and counting the stains on the floor to kill time. Aidan has been gone for eight hours. Selfish, irrational panic is replaced by genuine concern, but I force myself not to pace the ward. The old gents Aidan and I share our space with are settling down for the evening. I don't want to disturb them.

Or maybe it's that I can't face the empty bay where his bed should be.

Whatever.

I go back to ruminating over his money problems, and sometime after my dinner tray is collected, I have an epiphany.

My phone is dead and buried at the bottom of my bag. I dig it out and plug it into my portable charger. In my contacts list, I find the number for the employment adviser who handles my disability benefits and copy it onto a page I tear out of my empty journal. On its own it doesn't mean much, so I scrawl a note on the other side.

Aidan,

This lady helped me get a job and keep my house. Her name is Rachel.

Ludo

I fold the piece of paper into a perfect triangle and slide off my bed. *I can leave it on his table.* It's the most sensible idea I've had in weeks.

Adrenaline pumping, I yank socks onto my bare feet, tuck my aching arm into the sling I keep forgetting to use, and set off for

Aidan's bed bay, all the while bracing myself for confirmation that he *still isn't there.*

But as I get closer to Aidan's faraway corner, I realise that my pep talks have been for nothing. There is no empty space.

Aidan is back.

EIGHT

Aidan

Ever since I woke up in this damn-fucking place, confusion and pain have been my constant companions, but as I open my eyes and see Ludo heading towards me, somehow, he grounds me. The confusion is gone.

Shame I can't say the same for the pain. It's *everywhere*, as though the surgeon has taken a hammer to every joint in my body because drilling into my knee and thigh wasn't enough. Only the anti-emetic I begged for in recovery is stopping me vomiting all over myself. I can't deny it—I'm a fucking wreck.

Ludo ghosts around my curtain. He tucks something into my drawer and then his gaze settles on me, piercing and yet comforting. I want him to look at me for as long as possible so I can look at him.

"You're back," he says after a minute.

I make a sound low in my throat, half moan, half grunt.

Ludo treats me to a fleeting, magical touch—a brush of fingers down my forearm. "You've been gone ages. I thought you'd died."

I can't tell if he's being serious, but I imagine he is. Ludo doesn't joke much. He is honest and earnest, and nice—basically my opposite. "I . . ." I pause to moisten my cracked lips. "I didn't die. Just wish I had."

Ludo stills, and his gaze sharpens. "Don't say that."

"But it's true."

"It's not, or you wouldn't be living."

I'm too addled for this conversation, but somehow, through the nightmare my life has become, I know I've fucked up. "Ludo."

His name is all I have, and it comes out as a plea. Red-hot spikes are being jammed into every part of my body and I need him to stop frowning at me the way he is right now—as though I'm an unexploded bomb he's not sure he wants to dodge. As though he wants my pain to be his pain because he deserves it more than I do.

Fucking psychic, are you?

Hell no. But I apparently consider myself an expert on what Ludo is thinking, despite the fact he's never, ever told me.

Twat.

Ludo's silence is deafening. For a long moment, I fear he'll leave, but then he sags and drops into the chair I've come to think of as his. "You're in pain."

It's not a question. He knows. He touches my arm again, and I barely contain the shiver that will make me hurt a thousand times more.

I focus on his icy fingertips and note that he's wearing only a T-shirt and pyjama bottoms. The baggy hoody he usually wears is missing, and though his cool touch is soothing, I can't bear the thought that he might be cold.

As if on cue, he shivers, and I realise he's trembling, digging his teeth into his bottom lip to keep his jaw still.

Fuck this. "In the cabinet," I grind out.

"What?"

"My hoodie. Put it on."

"Why?"

"You're cold."

"I like it."

It takes me a moment to compute his words. And even then it doesn't work. *Nope. Not doing it.* "Please."

Ludo sighs and rises from his seat, using his uninjured arm to lever himself upright. "I'm only doing it to stop you having a tantrum."

His choice of words is so legit ridiculous I laugh, and it *hurts*, but it feels good.

Seeing his slight frame dwarfed by my huge hooded sweatshirt feels even better, and for the first time, I'm grateful to the paramedic who plucked it free from Bernard's ruined van. It's all I have, and I want Ludo to have it.

Ludo returns to his seat. He doesn't touch me again, but I don't mind. He's warm, and that's enough for me until another wave of pain eclipses any coherent thoughts I have left.

I groan as my body tightens to fight it. Tension ripples through me, adding to the jackhammer in my bones. This shit is insane. I can't take it.

Cool fingers brush my forehead, easing my hair back from my face. They've lost their icy edge but none of their magic. "Shh," Ludo whispers. "It'll get better, I promise."

But I don't believe him. The surgeon warned me I'd have a rough twenty-four hours after the surgery, and it's barely started. If anything, it'll get worse, and my morphine pump is empty.

I clench my fists and grind my teeth. *I can't do this.*

"You can," Ludo counters, letting me know I've spoken the words aloud. "If you survived that fall, you can survive anything."

"It should've killed me."

"But it didn't."

It's an incomplete echo of our previous exchange, but when I open my eyes, Ludo doesn't seem angry anymore. Just worried. And I hate that I've made him frown again, all the while my heart skips a beat for the fact that he's worried about *me*. That he cares, for reasons only he understands.

Ludo

I don't think I've ever seen anyone suffer like Aidan is right now, and worse than that, I can't see how he's ever going to get better when he has nothing but pain to keep him company.

He dozes in fits and starts. When he's awake, we talk. Well, I do, and he listens, and while he's sleeping, I study his barren bed bay with building unease. There's literally nothing here—a water jug, a couple of folded T-shirts, and a hoodie that *I'm* wearing. He has no phone, no books or magazines, and until last night he didn't know how to access a TV. *What does he do all day?*

But I already know the answer. He thinks and wishes he could stop.

Been there, mate.

I'm still there, but Aidan isn't like me. He can probably read a book without the narrator taking up residence in his head for a week after. Scan a newspaper without fretting for the rest of the day about impending nuclear war. I study his hands—hardened and scarred—and wonder what he likes to do with them when he's not climbing trees.

My brain is like a malfunctioning kitchen sink. Sometimes I turn the tap on and nothing happens. Others the sink fills so fast with ideas that I'm scrabbling for the plug to catch them all. It's late when Aidan's morphine pump reloads. He takes every drop available and finally falls into a sleep deep enough to last more than ten minutes. His hand is wrapped, like a baby's, around my index finger. For long minutes I can't bring myself to pull away, but then the sink threatens to overflow, and I know I must before every scrap of good intention is washed away.

I retreat from his bed and back to my own. My bag is stuffed in my bedside cabinet. I dig it out and rummage through it, emptying the contents onto my bed. Notebooks and pencils. A crime novel my neighbour gave me that I'll never read. There's even a newspaper, though it's days old, and it's the kind of newspaper no one admits to buying. Me? I bought it for the crossword . . . honest.

Regardless, it'll do. I pile it all up and traipse back to Aidan. He hasn't moved—he's more immobile than ever—but I linger a moment anyway. Though I know it's the morphine that's smoothed the lines of pain from his face, that he has months of recovery to endure, his peaceful expression is everything.

But I still have work to do. I dump my first bounty load in the chair by his bed and set off again.

"I'm hungry," I say when the night sister questions why I'm leaving the ward. "I want some chocolate from the kiosk."

She lets me go, and I shuffle through the hospital with socked feet until I come to the all-night shop by the A & E department.

There's a different vibe in this part of the hospital, a frenetic energy that sets my teeth on edge the moment it hits me. Sirens. Pacing relatives. Blood-soaked patients stacked up in chairs. I've never been to this A & E, but sordid déjà vu prickles my skin, and I picture how Aidan must've looked when he was first brought in—leg smashed up, bleeding from his head, and unconscious. Or maybe he wasn't—maybe he was awake and afraid. I don't know how that feels . . . to be hurt and scared of what that means. For me, every injury has been a relief.

He's not like you.

Of course he's not.

I speed-walk past the A & E waiting area and reach the kiosk. Even at this hour, there's a queue, and by the time I get to the front, I'm sweating, anxiety pouring out of me so fast I half expect my feet to get wet. I grab chocolate, sweets, and every magazine I can think of that isn't a bullshit gossip rag. Gardening, photography, fishing. On my way back to the ward, I question the wisdom of gifting Aidan a fitness magazine and dump *Men's Health* in the bin.

At his bedside again, I stack his entertainment stash on the table. It doesn't seem enough, but the itch to go back and buy more brings the worst parts of me to life, so I stamp it down and flee.

Back in my own bed, I realise that I've forgotten to say goodnight or leave a note explaining the corner shop I've dumped on his bedside table. Panic seizes me again, but a nurse is doing the rounds, and a stern glare from her keeps me in bed.

She lingers on purpose, apparently finding the contents of a nearby patient's chart fascinating enough to sit down and read it. Heart thumping, I curl up in Aidan's oversized hoodie, drawing it tight around me, hood up, until I'm surrounded by enough of his clean, woodsy scent that my pulse slows and my racing thoughts even out.

I fall asleep.

It's morning when I wake, and Aidan is my first thought. I scramble out of bed and dash through the ward to get to him, only to find that he's still asleep, and my collection of things that now seem ridiculous are exactly as I left them.

The urge to gather them up and hurl them in the nearest bin is strong, but my nurse nemesis from the night before is preparing to leave the nurse station.

I take my chance and slope back to my own bed.

When I get there, the surgeon is waiting for me, and Dr Farsi is with him.

NINE

Aidan

Four months later . . .

I'm twenty-six years old and my summer has been reduced to sitting on a bench in my tiny garden, wishing there was a bus that ran from my shitty bedsit to the pub . . . or at least the return journey. Apparently, I forget my leg doesn't work right when I've had a skin full, and I have new scars on my face to prove it.

Loser.

But that's hardly news. I was a basket case before the accident.

Sighing, I tilt my face to the sun and wish its warmth would seep into my aching bones. I've been cold for months, and even the steamiest day of the year so far isn't enough to ease the chill I brought home from the hospital. I shiver and knock my head against the brick wall behind me, but all that does is remind me of the many times I watched Ludo do the same thing on his bed rail, and a new wave of melancholy hits me.

Because that's the other thing: it doesn't seem to matter how much I drink or how many pills I pop, Ludo's imprint on me is permanent. There's not a single word, touch, or exchanged glance I can't remember with perfect clarity, and it's killing me.

The nurse won't leave. She's bustling around my bed, piling up the books, magazines, and junk food that have materialised while I've been in a morphine coma. She says I look better already, that I'll be up on my feet in no time.

I want to punch her.

At the very least, I want her to fuck off so I can figure out what the hell is going on. If it weren't for the throbbing pain in my leg, I'd have thought I was dreaming, but even through the morphine haze, I remember the world I closed my eyes to.

Ludo was here. With me. He touched my hand and talked to me. For hours. And in this moment, all that matters to me is that he's not here now.

The nurse leaves, and I raise my bed to a sitting position, pressing my fist into my mouth to muffle my groan. There are a dozen magazines piled up on the bedside cabinet and even more chocolate bars. I flick through the magazines with a deepening frown until I come to Gardeners' Weekly. *Something clicks, and a chuckle bursts out of me as I read the cover teaser about diseased oaks. It's all from Ludo; it has to be. He's probably the only person who's ever listened to me rant about trees without rolling his eyes or heard my confession regarding my addiction to Snickers bars.*

Footsteps approach my bed. My heart leaps, but I glance up to meet the gaze of the same nurse who's just left.

"Mr Drummond?"

"What?"

The nurse doesn't flinch. With a knowing smile that feels so fucking smug, she hands me my hoodie and a scrap of paper folded into a tiny triangle.

It's from Ludo.

He's gone.

I return to the present with a sharp gasp, and my hand moves of its own accord to rub my chest, as though it can plug the inexplicable hole there. After that day, I didn't take a single hit of morphine the entire time I was in hospital, and I fought sleep as though it was my worst enemy in case Ludo came back.

But the self-inflicted exhaustion did me no good. Physiotherapy took longer and hurt more than it should've done, and *Ludo didn't come back.*

That hurt more than it should've done too.

Still hurt. And I don't know why. I learnt that damn-fucking note by heart, and every day I have to convince myself that the impersonal goodbye he left me doesn't mean anything, that my attachment to him is a symptom of some fucked up cabin fever. But every day, I fail. Either Ludo is a morphine-induced hallucination or the current between us is real—*still* real, even though he left me without any means to track him down. No number, no address, no full name to stalk him on social media. And trust me, I've tried, though recently I've made a resolution to drink more instead.

With another sigh, I haul myself inside and limp to the fridge. The beer bottle feels warm to my cold hands, but I open it and drink it in one swallow anyway. Regret courses through me before I set the bottle down, but I shrug it off and shuffle to the sofa where I've left the cheap whisky. I want to sleep, but the fear of waking up keeps me conscious. Before the accident, I slept hard, deep, and all night long, waking only to the second alarm I set on my phone. Now I sleep for a couple of hours, and the slightest noise—imagined or real—disturbs me. I panic and, every fucking time, come awake certain that I'm falling all over again.

Whisky helps. Sometimes.

It doesn't help today. I drink enough to put me into a coma, and yet somehow I'm still bolt upright on my couch, suffocating in my crappy bedsit. The whisky courses through my veins, but instead of slumber, it stokes a fire I can't ignore. Even the empty bottle makes my heart beat too fast. Because . . . *Ludo*. Because every-fucking-thing reminds me of him, no matter how tenuous a connection my ridiculous brain dreams up.

With the whisky, it's simple. I buy it with the money Bernard has deposited in my bank account every week since the accident. The money *Ludo* suggested he'd feel guilty enough to pay me. It's enough that I don't even need to call the number Ludo left in my drawer, but I keep the note anyway, along with the bland goodbye. I keep both tucked into my wallet, and I can't see how I'll ever throw them away.

Yeah. That's right. I'm clinging to scraps of paper to validate my obsession with a dude who was likely nice to me because he was bored.

Loser. I close my eyes and repeat the insult over and over, but while acceptance of who I've become sometimes grants me respite, today, as the afternoon sun fades to a gold-hued evening, a terminal restlessness steals over me. However much it hurts to move, I can't sit still.

I abandon the whisky bottle and make for the door. The pub calls my name, but I turn in the opposite direction and just fucking *walk*, pain dulled by booze and apathy until I can't feel a thing in my mashed-up leg. It's odd like that. As though the nerves have given up on me as much as everyone else.

Not Michael though. But I push all thoughts of my earnest cousin away. I can't think about him without a shed-load of guilt, and I'm enjoying my moment of nothingness.

Eventually, my aimless wander takes me to the edge of town. In the distance I can see the railway bridge and the hills. In front of me are the woods I ran riot through as a teenager—drinking, banging powder, and smoking weed. I miss those times, but the tiny part of me that is a responsible adult cringes at the damage I might've caused the trees.

The woods are vast and populated by ash and sweet chestnut, but there's a broad oak close to the heathland that, for many years, was the biggest tree I'd ever seen.

Fuck it.

I push on into the woods, treading carefully over uneven ground. The woods are popular with dog walkers and children, but I see no one. Hear nothing but birds and rustling leaves. It's heaven and the closest to climbing I can be right now, so I keep walking and walking until I reach the gargantuan tree from my childhood.

It's not that tall, but it's wide—ten metres in girth. There are many bigger trees in the world, but in my little corner, this old girl is fucking mystical. I make a loop around her huge trunk, fingers trailing rough bark, and for the first time in weeks, I feel something of myself return to me.

Perhaps it's not Ludo I've been missing after all. Perhaps it's myself.

TEN

Ludo

If anyone ever tells you it's a good idea for an overly anxious person to get a dog, I'm telling you right now, it's not. Or maybe it is, but it's a bloody nightmare for *me*.

Bella eats my couch and chews my shoes.

Bella leaves slobber on my walls and hair on my bed.

Bella licks my windows and steals actual rubbish from the bin.

Bella is a golden retriever. She makes me go out when I want to stay in, and I love her so much it scares me.

And *there's* the problem I've always had with loving things . . . people, animals, whichever. With love comes fear of living without it. Of breaking it. Hurting it. Of doing the wrong thing, like I've done over and over my entire life.

Oblivious to the riot going on in my head, Bella paws my knee, sad gaze drifting to the window and back. She wants to run, but she doesn't realise how hot it's been today, how many articles I've read about dogs dying from heat exhaustion, and how terrified I am that something will happen to her if we go out before the sun goes down.

I scratch her ears and press my face to hers. "Not yet."

Bella returns my solemn stare and I'm convinced she understands every word. She ambles away to the den I've built her under the stairs and the bed she only sleeps in during the day. At night she sleeps with me, star-shaped on my bed, legs in the air like a beached turtle, and I like it cos I know she's happy.

I take a deep breath and return my attention to my computer screen and the work I have to get done by the end of the day. It's software testing and boring as hell, but the monotony is good for me. And flexible contracts mean I can work when I'm well and take unlimited time off when I'm . . . not.

But you are well now.

I steal a glance at Bella and search for the spark of joy that's sometimes bright enough to silence the counter argument from the devil.

Yeah, but for how long?

As if speculating when my current state of sanity will expire ever does me a blind bit of good.

I turn back to my work and lose myself in the dull activity of repeating the same task, over and over, and recording the results. It kills time, but my mind wanders, and when my wrist begins to ache, I know, deadline or not, I'm done for the day.

Stop it.

But I can't. The throb in my wrist has nothing to do with where my brain wants to go and everything to do with the eight hours I've spent at my computer today, but I'm somehow unable to stop the giant leap back in time.

My living room disappears, the scents of cut grass and the toast I burnt at lunchtime replaced by nuked food and disinfectant. The summer sun warming my house becomes a stiff winter breeze, and Bella's quiet company is someone else.

In the fragment of my mind that's still in the present, I wonder if Aidan would mind being compared to a dog, if he'd find it funny. Then I recall the two times he actually smiled and figure he likely wouldn't give a shit, and a shudder passes through me.

You don't know those smiles were even real.

It's true. I'm confident enough that I haven't invented him, but the details . . . I have no clue. A lot has happened since I was hauled off the regular ward to spend a week in the psychiatric unit. Highs. Lows. Yellows and blacks. I'm in a distinctly beige state of mind at the moment, which makes thinking easier, but *remembering* is always tricky. All I can recall for certain about Aidan is that I can't entirely forget him.

And that I can't decide if I want to.

Bella whines, dragging me back to a reality I can trust. I turn my gaze to her and admit defeat with a heavy sigh. "All right, girl. You win."

As a rule, when the colours I can see are more light than dark, I like being out of my house. People, fresh air, moving my rickety limbs . . . it's all good for my soul, man. But the woods where Bella loves to run are more of a challenge than a stroll down the high street, especially when the sun fades and most people go home.

Solitude. Silence. It's too loud, and I fight to keep my anxiety down. To keep my safe place from being sucked into the never-ending space before me. I have tools, though. The gorgeous scenery, Bella's contagious excitement, and a quick glance to the railway bridge on the horizon—a stark reminder of how bad things can get when I don't pay attention.

I tighten my grip on Bella's lead. "Come on, girl. Let's go."

We venture into the woods, past the bird watching outpost and the timber stores. Bella's favourite path takes us on the longest route ever, but I don't mind. Without her, I'd miss the low sun melting through the trees and the squirrels laughing at her from the highest branches. And it *does* feel good to move my body. My ankles feel strong, and the aches and pains in my other abused bones fade.

My appreciation of that is something too. For now, the days where I welcomed pain as a hearty distraction are somewhere else, and despite missing Aidan more than I can ever explain, I'm okay with that.

I have to be.

We keep walking. I throw dead branches and pinecones for Bella to chase and even a stick into the shallow part of the lake. I'm petrified she'll drown, but of course, she doesn't. She's a better swimmer than most humans, and she's back before my heart combusts, shaking water and mud all over me.

"Git."

I toss the stick into the thickly carpeted woodland and follow her there, hoping she'll dry off before I have a soggy dog on my bed to deal with. It's almost as though she doesn't believe I can make enough of my own mess.

If only she knew.

Bella charges ahead, paying little attention to my commands for her to wait. I trail after her, cursing the friendly psych nurse who thought adding this to my day would be healthy. My tentative good mood turns to irritation until I reach the top of the hill and see Bella at the bottom, paused majestically in a dappled glade.

I can never be cross with her for long.

Shaking my head, I fish a treat from my pocket and scramble down the hill. She waits for me this time, naturally. I reach her and offer her the reward. She takes the squishy, meaty lump and turns her gaze forwards again. I absently follow her line of sight to the copse a few metres away—trees, undergrowth, and neat piles of sticks from the local boy scouts. Nothing I haven't seen before, but something makes me look twice, and that's when I really see it.

See *him*—the broad-shouldered figure sitting at the foot of a tree trunk. He rises slowly, like he's been sitting for a long time, and his long body unravels like an uncoiling snake. His eyes find mine, and for a brief, heart-stopping moment, I think it's Aidan, but it's not. It can't be. The Aidan I remember has short hair and lies flat on his back. He doesn't stand tall in my enchanted forest, dwarfed only by the enormous tree behind him.

ELEVEN

Aidan

Bernard has been spiking the whisky in the local shop. He knows it's my favourite vice when I'm in a shit mood, and lacing it with LSD is his revenge for every scrap of disrespect I've shown him over the years.

Yeah. That's it. It has to be . . . it's the only rational explanation I can think of for the apparition that's appeared in front of me in the shape of the world's cutest dog and the man who's haunted my thoughts every moment I'm not blind drunk.

I blink hard and push my overlong hair out of my face, willing the vision to disappear despite the fact that I've spent many long nights fantasising about a moment just like this. Because that's all it is—a fantasy. Ludo isn't from around here. There's no logical reason for him to be strolling through *my* damn-fucking woods.

The dog starts towards me.

"*Bella.*"

And I blink again as the impact of the softly uttered word hits me. Have you ever felt as though the world has stopped turning? Cos that's how I feel right now. I never knew Ludo's face as well as I wanted to, but I learnt his voice—every rise and fall, the smooth bits and the sharp edges. It's how I knew him . . . how I *know* him. *Oh god, it's really him.*

I step forward, but the dog responds before I can take a breath. It bounds over a fallen trunk and dashes away, it's golden fur merging with fading sunlight until I can't be sure where one ends and the other begins.

And then it's gone, and Ludo is too, and I'm alone again, like I've always been, like I always *was* until I met him.

He's not real. You're drunk and tired. Go home.

For a long moment, I attempt to make peace with common sense, but as my heart beats a frantic tattoo, hammering my ribcage, I don't care what's real and what's not. I care about Ludo, and as ridiculous as I *fucking know* it is, I miss him.

Follow him.

But it's easier thought than done. My drunken hike has taken its toll on my broken body and I can't walk without dragging my stiff leg behind me. Returning my sorry arse to the uneven forest floor is so fucking tempting, but my body keeps going, limping towards the light in the fashion of an escapee from the set of *The Walking Dead.*

It hurts. I stumble so many times I take the skin off my knuckles steadying myself on fortuitously placed trees, but I don't stop. I *can't*, and my dumb-fuck naïve self is so utterly convinced that Ludo will be waiting for me when I emerge from the woods that it takes me a full minute to reconcile myself with the fact that he isn't.

Of course he isn't. I stumble through the gate to the same quiet lane as when I arrived, and energy drains from me like water through a sieve.

You daft cunt.

I sag against the gatepost, grief and confusion crashing into me in a tidal wave of humiliating perspective. The buzz of my whisky binge has faded to a dry mouth and a headache, and I'm not altogether sure how I got here. The woods are a mile from my bedsit. Add in the trudge to the magical tree and back, and I've walked further today than I have since way before the accident.

I'm dead on my feet; I can't imagine how I'll ever get home. Or if I even want to . . . if I can face another night tossing and turning in bed until I inevitably give up and wind up outside, huddled on my bench as I wait for the sun to rise and give me a fucking break.

I don't want to do it . . . any of it. But I have to. I've got previous for kipping on the street, and though I'm a long way from being happily too drunk to care, the old bill around here dislike me enough to stop and ask questions.

A night in the cells would probably finish me off. *Fuck that shit.*

I push off the gatepost and start walking, forcing my battered leg to keep moving, dragging my toes along the pavement. A car passes me. For a hot second I allow myself to imagine that it's Ludo coming back for me, to drive me home, come inside and lock the doors so it's just me and him forever, then I figure myself even more of a weirdo than before, and blacking out in the street is suddenly a viable option again.

Somehow I reach the end of the lane. Across the road is a row of three houses and a disused phone box. It's a vintage one, painted red, still stuffed full of old-school calling cards. I can't believe it's still there, that it hasn't been vandalised or nicked, but then, this town isn't like that. The only idiot hooligan I can remember running the streets around here is me. And I can't fucking run now.

A hysterical laugh escapes me. I stumble against a dry-stone wall and cling to it as if I'm drowning. It's getting dark, and I welcome the shadows as they close in around me. Teenaged me was an idiot, and I'm an idiot still. For months I've existed for the sake of someone I'll never see again, waiting for some kind of fucking epiphany to save me. And because it hasn't happened, I've made one up. Got so messed up I'm seeing things in the one place I've always felt at home.

I need the woods. I need the trees. I can't let whatever car crash is happening in my brain take them away from me. I just *can't*—

"Aidan."

I close my eyes. "No."

Ludo

Sometimes the worst has to happen to make things right. I ran all the way home from the woods, threw Bella's dinner at her, and then sat in my living room window, fixated on the lane leading to the woods, convinced that if no one emerged after an hour or so, it was probably time to call Rita to come and rescue me.

It's rare that I'm able to pre-empt a crisis, that I have the foresight to warn the people paid to care about me that I'm not okay. For a little while I thought I cracked it, that this time and the next I'd be ready for whatever was coming.

But nothing could've prepared me for the sight of Aidan staggering out of the lane and collapsing against the wall. In a heartbeat, the blurred lines between real and illusion cease to matter. Real or not, Aidan needs me, and I sprint across the road, barefoot and frantic.

"Aidan."

"No." He shakes his head and buries his face in his hands. "You're not real. Leave me alone."

"I am real."

"You're not. You never were."

He's in my head. There's no other explanation for how he can echo my own thoughts verbatim. For how the struggle in him resonates so deeply in my consciousness that my hand shoots out to touch him before I can check myself.

I close my fingers around his bicep—a part of his arm I never touched in the hospital—and squeeze, to ground myself as much as him. "Aidan, I'm real, I promise. Just look at me . . . please?"

For a second I fear he won't. That I'll have to let go and leave him like this, and it will be a hundred times harder than leaving him in the hospital, but then he groans, an animalistic cry for help that cuts me to the bone, and raises his head.

And I barely recognise the face that stares back at me. I've never seen Aidan's bright blue eyes unmarred by pain and morphine, but months down the line, perhaps I've forgotten how much his injuries *hurt*. How sad and lonely he was, despite how hard he tried to hide it with indifference and anger.

My hand slides from his arm and I touch his face, just for a moment, grazing the dark shadows beneath his red-rimmed eyes. "You didn't get better."

He shakes his head. "But you did."

How does he know? Embarrassment ripples through me as I ponder what side of myself I showed him in the hospital. By my standards, the manic episode and subsequent crash were mild—crisis lite . . . diet crazy—but Aidan doesn't know me any better than I know myself. How can he know that right now, I'm as stable as I'm ever going to get?

This isn't about you.

Of course it isn't. And as the thought completes, Aidan sways on his feet. I steady him, wishing this wasn't the first time I've ever seen him upright. I wish he was happy and free and that it was easy to let him go. But he's not happy, and I knew that even before today. "Aidan." I try again. "Where are you trying to go? Do you live near here?"

He leans on me, though I can tell he doesn't mean to. That he wouldn't for one second if he realised. "I live round here," he says slowly, slurring, like he's drunk. "But you don't."

"What makes you say that?"

"Because I'd know."

"Would you?"

"Yeah."

I turn us round so we're facing the road, my arm still looped under his broad shoulders. "Then you don't know much. My house is right there, on the end."

"It's not."

"It is."

"It can't be."

"Why not?"

He's run out of answers, and energy, apparently. His legs give way and it takes every ounce of my strength to hold us both up. Lacking any better ideas, I manoeuvre him away from the wall and start walking.

"Where are we going?" he grunts.

"For a cup of tea," I say, even though I don't have any in my cupboards. "Then maybe I'll call you a cab to wherever you're supposed to be."

He doesn't answer, so I keep towing him until we reach my front door, wide open, as I left it when I charged across the road to get to him. I kick it shut and somehow manhandle Aidan into the kitchen, thankful I have the bad habit of leaving all the chairs untucked.

Aidan falls into one and instantly slumps over my cluttered kitchen table. One arm is flung out in front of him, the other tucked under his unshaven chin. His hair falls over his face. The urge to brush it back is so strong it takes my breath away, so I retreat to the kettle while I try and come to terms with the fact that the man I've been dreaming of is passed out in my kitchen.

It's a tough reality to swallow, and I almost don't, but then Bella comes in from the patio where she's been chomping on the stick she brought home from the woods and stops dead in the doorway, her standard reaction for the rare occasions someone she doesn't know comes into the house. She tilts her head sideways and sniffs the air. Then, clearly deciding she likes what she smells, she prances over to Aidan and treats him to an exuberant lick.

"What the—" He straightens so fast he must have given himself whiplash. He stares at Bella, and in slow motion, he drags his gaze to me. "I—I don't know what's happening."

I think of all the times I've stuttered those words at a well-meaning stranger and been even more terrified by their response. I think of the one and only time a stranger has ever managed to calm me.

"You are crazy, Ludo, but never forever. Everything always is fluid. Nothing sticks."

The student nurse was kicked off his course for repeated use of the term *crazy*. It's inappropriate, judgemental, and cruel, and for some shows a level of ignorance that can't be forgiven, *but* the word has never bothered *me*. It's *mine*, and I own it, and since that day I've never considered it a theme that can't be swapped out for something else.

I was unwell then and I will be again, but I'm not right now.

Aidan was unhappy when I met him and he still is, but that doesn't mean he has to be.

I cross the room and crouch in front of him, my hands on his knees, and I'm so sure I can feel the pins holding his bones together that I almost pull away.

But I don't pull away. I hold his gaze and smile enough to help him feel safe. "I think you're drunk and lost, in every sense of the word, so I'm going to make you some tea and some food. Then we can talk, and maybe I can help you get home."

TWELVE

Aidan

It's not often that I sober up to find my dreams have come true. Usually I'm face down on the carpet having rolled off my bed in the dead of night or, more recently, in the middle of the day.

This time, I come to my senses in a cosy kitchen I don't recognise, but it feels so fucking familiar, I can't help wondering if I've been here before.

Ludo doesn't say much. He mostly keeps his back to me as he makes hot chocolate—despite his promise, he actually doesn't have any tea—and rummages in his fridge for something to eat.

"You don't have to do that," I protest weakly. "I'm not hungry."

"Doesn't mean you shouldn't eat."

I don't argue. How can I when I'm ravenous for anything that allows me to see his face? Beneath it all, I'm so fucking embarrassed I want the ground to open up and swallow me whole, but *Ludo is here*, and nothing else matters. So I sit at his kitchen table as if I haven't downed a bottle of whisky and stumbled into his life like a pisshead loser.

Ludo cooks pasta with cherry tomatoes and basil grown in a pot on his windowsill. Spiked with olive oil and garlic, it's so delicious I hoover it up in ten seconds flat, leading him to reload my plate with the kind of smile I wish he wore all the time.

I clear my plate for a second time, then flop back in my seat and survey my surroundings. With a full belly and the sugar from the hot chocolate working its way through my system, everything seems clearer, and I take a nosy glance around Ludo's kitchen as though I'm seeing it for the first time.

It's small, chaotic, and lovely. The appliances are old and battered, the wooden table chipped and weathered, and despite the fact that he's probably younger than me, it suits him. Until this moment, I've never seen Ludo look as if he *belongs* somewhere.

He catches me staring. "What?"

I shrug. "I like your kitchen."

"Why?"

I consider voicing the thoughts that have just passed through my head, but when I open my mouth, nothing comes out, and I shrug again.

Ludo has never pushed me to answer questions. I reckon it's a defensive measure because he needs me to give him the same space, but it's hard when all I want is to know absolutely everything about him.

It's my turn to speak, but I settle for running my gaze over him, absorbing the changes that have taken place since I last saw him—not that I can truly remember much of that. But I do remember his dark circled eyes and painfully thin frame. The terrified shadows haunting his gaze, and the way he was so shrunken into himself it was as though he wanted to die.

Or maybe I don't remember it and it's more that in comparison with the Ludo in front of me now, it's so fucking obvious.

Ludo is leaning on the counter, unfazed by my scrutiny. It's almost as if he expects it. I wonder why, but the thought is too complicated for my hungover brain, so I don't pursue it. Instead I give way to my craving for a better look and beckon Ludo closer.

He smirks and pushes himself off the counter. "Having trouble with your hearing again?"

"Huh?"

"In the hospital . . . you made me come over to you because you couldn't hear me."

"I don't remember that."

"Probably for the best. You were in a lot of pain."

I get what he's saying, but the idea that I had conversations with him that I can't recall upsets me in ways I can't explain. Already my Ludo bank is too low, and I've given up contemplating what it says about me that it even exists. "I can hear you fine," I say. "I'm just hoping you'll sit with me."

Ludo drops into the nearest chair. "I thought you might want some space. I haven't been drunk in forever, but the end game always lands me feeling pretty claustrophobic."

Claustrophobic. I turn the word over, trying it on for size, but it's impossible for me to feel like that when Ludo is so close. I file it away for later when I'm trapped in my bedsit again with just my miserable self for company. "Are you allowed to drink . . . I mean, with your, er, bipolar?"

"Were you going to call it a disease, Aidan?"

"What? No, course I wasn't. I'm just a fucking mess and struggling to find any fucking words, let alone the right ones."

It comes out as a slurred mess. Perhaps I'm not as sober as I feel. But Ludo smiles faintly and finally—*finally*—lays his magic hand on my arm. "It's okay. I was taking the piss . . . out of myself, and you. I don't care what you call it."

"I'm not calling it anything."

"I know."

"So . . . are you allowed to drink? Or does it make it worse for you?"

"Depends." Ludo sketches a picture on my forearm. "I can technically drink with the medication I'm on, but I have to be super careful, and when I'm in the mood to drink, it's usually when being super careful isn't at the top of my list. I've made myself really sick in the past, so I try to avoid it."

I don't know jack about bipolar. A few lonely nights have driven me to google that shit, but every article I read was different, and I'm no wiser than I was when we met. "I wish I didn't drink."

"Are you an alcoholic?"

It's not the first time I've been asked that question. "I don't know. I mean, I'm not physically addicted—I didn't miss it when I was in hospital—but it didn't take me long to get back on it once I was home."

"Uh-huh." Ludo draws another picture. Scribbles it out and tries again. His fingertip on my skin is giving me goosebumps but somehow feels so normal I can almost ignore it.

Almost.

"I've always been a caner," I say when Ludo doesn't speak. "My dad gave me my first beer when I was ten and I lost my stop button somewhere in my teens."

"How old are you?"

"How old are *you*? I can't work it out."

Ludo snorts. "Twenty-five, but I got asked for ID buying fags a few months ago, so maybe I don't look it."

"You smoke?"

"Sometimes."

"Is it like the drinking thing? You only do it in self-destruct mode?"

"Something like that."

"They told me not to smoke after surgery. Said I'd get gangrene or some shit. So I haven't."

Ludo reclaims his finger and stands. He sweeps my plate and mug from the table and carries them to the sink. "You smoked a lot before?"

"Like a fucking chimney."

"Then you *do* have willpower."

He turns the tap on and fills the sink. I wonder if I should go or help him with the dishes, but I don't move. I just watch him, tracking every movement in his slender body. Yeah, cos despite the fact that he's gained some weight since I last saw him, he's still a skinny mofo. He's lost the blond though. His hair is now as dark as mine and almost as long.

It suits him. And I'm digging his clothes—slouchy ripped jeans and a faded black tee with the sleeves rolled up. He's barefoot too, which is my fucking kryptonite, but I shove that vibe down. Ludo does things to me no one else ever has, but I haven't had a sexual thought in so long that I no longer know what to do with them.

I draw my gaze away from his perfect feet and back to the pale skin of his exposed arms. The masochist in me searches for his surgery scar, curious if it's as macabre as mine, but I stop short before I get to his wrist.

Jesus.

In the hospital, Ludo wore huge T-shirts, and on the isolated occasion he didn't, I was too fucked up to scrutinise him too hard before I gave him my own. Now, though, I wish I had because it would mean that the white lines covering his biceps and inner arms wouldn't be brand new to me. That the shock sluicing through me would've already happened, and the churning in my stomach and the scraping sensation in my heart would be in the past.

I shove my chair back, on my feet before I truly know what I'm doing. Six months ago I'd have crossed the kitchen in one stride, but I'm clumsy now and weak, and Ludo hears me coming.

He turns as I reach him. "Aidan . . ."

But his words die on his lips as I seize his arm and gently extend it so I can see every inch of his brutalised skin. The white lines are *everywhere*. The only punctuation is the thick pink line from his surgery. "What—" I stop. Take a breath. Try again. "How many of these do you have?"

Ludo turns his bottomless gaze on me. "How many what? Scars in total? Or by my own hand?"

"I don't know."

"Then you shouldn't ask." He twists his arm out of my grasp but makes no move to get away from me. "Either way, I stopped counting a long time ago."

"Do you, uh, still do it?"

"Cut myself? Don't be coy, Aidan."

Coy. There's a word I haven't ever heard in real life. "Sorry. Okay. Do you still cut yourself?"

"No. Not at the moment. I'd imagine it's like your drinking—a security blanket when I forget any other ways of coping with life.

Most of those marks are years old, but I can't promise I'll never make any new ones."

It makes more sense than I want it to. I take Ludo's arm again and examine a particularly grisly scar on the underside of his bicep. I rub my thumb over it, as though I can push it back inside him and spare him the pain, but of course I can't. I can't do anything but wish life had been easier for him. For both of us so we weren't huddled in his kitchen on this balmy evening, trying desperately to understand each other.

I let his arm drop. I want to know where else he has scars, but in this moment, I vow that I'll never ask. That anything he shares with me is because he *wants* to, not because I've backed him into a corner and taken what *I* need. "I'm sorry."

"Why?"

"Because life is shit and you deserve better."

"You don't know that."

"Convince me you don't."

"Works both ways."

"Does it?"

Ludo shrugs. "I think so."

It's enough . . . for now. And I know it's time to go. I nudge our shoulders together. "I should get home."

"Got someone waiting for you?"

"What do you think?"

"I think you're not enjoying your own company as much as you thought you would."

"Psychic bastard."

"I've been called worse."

I laugh. Ludo does too, and it wakes his dog who's been sleeping by the back door. She gets up and pads over to us, shouldering her way between us. I take it as my final cue and back off.

It takes me a minute to get my bearings and find the front door. Ludo follows me to the hallway. "Have you got far to go?"

I don't want to think about how long it will take me to get home. I grunt, non-committal and vague, my very best qualities. "I'll be okay. Thanks for the food. It was great."

"Uh-huh."

Ludo doesn't sound convinced, so I turn to face him. He's leaning on the doorframe, a worried frown marring his face.

"It *was*. Whatever your fretting about, forget it."

"How do you know I'm fretting?"

"Intuition." I turn back to the door and open it. I have one foot outside when Ludo calls my name. "What?"

"Just so you know," he says. "I've never cooked for anyone, and I hate having people in my house."

"What's different about me?"

He smiles, just a little. "Everything."

THIRTEEN

Ludo

I have no idea where to find Aidan. He left without telling me where he lived, or his number, and I didn't think to ask. Why would I when the only contacts in my phone are years out of date or that of mental health professionals paid to make sure I don't die?

You're in a morbid mood. I can't deny it, but part of my rehabilitation has always been to challenge my negative thoughts, and I can't think of a solution to my reactivated obsession with Aidan.

So I stop trying and worry about his welfare instead. Aidan is a beautiful man, but there's no getting away from the fact that when he was slumped at my kitchen table, he looked like absolute hell. Tired, drunk, and so depressed I feared he'd gone back in time, found *me* from two years ago, and stepped inside my threadbare skin.

Yeah, cos he'd want to do that after he saw the wreckage on your arms.

My scars tingle. I rub my hands up and down them, but it's no good. I'm indelibly marked by Aidan's touch, and the empathy in his eyes as he studied my ruined skin will stay with me forever.

He understands.

It's an impossible thought. Aidan doesn't know me. But I believe it and take another step out of my house. I'm going into town. All morning I've told myself it's because I need stuff from the shops, not because I'm looking for Aidan, but I'm far from convinced. I order my groceries online specifically for the reason that I'll never go hungry if I can't leave my house. And my cupboards are stocked. There's no reason for me to go into town.

I'll have to think of one on the way.

The walk into town takes me exactly twelve minutes. By the time I reach the high street, I remember that I *do* have a reason to be there—my fortnightly meeting with my community psychiatric nurse.

Rita is my CPN. I see her once a month when I'm super well, every day when I'm not. Every two weeks is the best I've had it in a long time, though, and I'm happy with that. Rita makes me smile, especially when she brings me big fat slices of her Jamaican black cake.

"You need some real food in you, boy," she comments fondly as I devour one slice straight away and stash the other in my bag for later. "A man can't survive on pasta."

"It's all I can cook. Lucky for me I know a hundred different ways, eh?"

I don't mention that I haven't cooked since I brought Aidan home, that I've been surviving on leftovers and toast . . . or that I haven't put his plate back in the cupboard. Washing it was as far as I got, and even that took me a couple of days.

You're cray cray, mate.

"Ludo?"

"Hmm?"

I glance at Rita. She's watching me like she does, unobtrusively analysing everything about me, not just what I say. Or what I don't. She's better at this than any psychiatrist, more intuitive in her work than her nurse's salary deserves.

"What are you ruminating about?" she asks. "Has something happened?"

"I'm not ruminating."

My denial is pointless, but I do it anyway, because it's part of the game. Much of me still resents having to flay my life open to cope with it, and I can't help staging a weak final protest.

Rita sits back in her seat. She hasn't eaten any cake, but an open packet of rich tea biscuits is on her desk. Her gaze flits to them, and I smile. "I thought you were laying off the biscuits before your holiday?"

She sighs. "I was, but complicated patients like you will drive any woman to eat."

"I'm not complicated."

"Of course you're not. So tell me what's got you speculative?"

I cave, like I've learnt to do, and tell her everything. She already knows about Aidan anyway—I told her about him when she came to visit me in the psychiatric hospital, though I don't know if she checked he actually existed before she persuaded the hospital team to let me go.

I'd be lying if I didn't admit that suspecting she might've done went a long way towards *me* believing he existed. But I'm so done with the *Is he real?* conundrum that I cut the thought dead and keep going with the truth.

"I don't think he's very well."

Rita caves and snags a biscuit. "Physically or mentally?"

"Both."

"That's hardly surprising. He's been through a lot. But what in particular do you think is wrong with him?"

I curl my legs and tuck my feet beneath me. "I don't think he's looking after himself, because I don't think he cares. I *think* he drinks a lot and doesn't eat enough, and there's no one around to help him get better."

"Well, you know how that feels," Rita says carefully. "And you've always managed to get better. Do you think you'll see him again?"

"I don't know. I mean, he didn't tell me if he lives around here, and I didn't get his number or anything, so maybe I won't."

"How do you feel about that?"

My mind is so completely on Aidan that I've forgotten that Rita's vested interest in the conversation is me. That Aidan's fate—if it doesn't affect *my* mental health—is of no consequence to her. It isn't her fault; it's her job, but I resent it anyway. There are already too many people in the world who don't care about Aidan.

Or are there? I think of his cousin—Michael—and wonder what became of him. If he ever came to visit Aidan again after Aidan sent him away.

"*Ludo*."

Oops. I blink and focus on Rita. "Yeah?"

"I want to know how you feel about the possibility that you might not see Aidan again. Is it something that worries you?"

"Yes," I say without hesitation, because it's true. "I'm worried that if I don't see him, no one will, and he'll never be okay."

"But why does that matter to you? You hardly know him."

But for once, Rita is wrong. I do know Aidan. And he does matter.

Still, the possibility that I'll never see him again is as hard to ignore as it was before he appeared in the woods by my house, and I face up to it because I have to. I leave Rita and take the scenic walk home, avoiding the high street altogether. I've never been a believer in fate, but while the logical part of my brain is working, I have to embrace it.

If Aidan and I are meant to cross paths again, we will. I can't reprogramme my life to force it.

I push him as far from my mind as he's ever likely to get and concentrate on planning the walk Bella and I will take tonight when the sun fades. When we weren't discussing Aidan, Rita encouraged me to take Bella swimming more. There's a man-made lake half a mile from my house, shallow and popular enough that there's always someone around. I'll take her there. After all, it's not as though *I* can't swim . . . right?

As ever, I have little idea where I'm going with my thoughts, but as I reach the quiet street by the council offices, they taper off.

Of course they do, because the moment I've given up on searching for Aidan, there he is, coming out of the off-licence with a full bag of bottles and a newspaper tucked under his arm.

FOURTEEN

Aidan

I sense him before I see him. My gaze seeks him out before I know I'm looking for him, and it's the weirdest sensation I've dealt with for a while.

It's shocking too, because I've spent the last week fighting the urge to knock on his door, to present myself to him as a lost cause and beg him to help me, even though I *fucking know* he has enough bullshit of his own to deal with.

Not that I think bipolar is bullshit. I'm just rubbish at expressing myself using more than six words. And I don't want him to help me. I just know that the time I spent in his house that I can actually remember is the safest I've felt in years.

You have no right to feel that way.

I know that too.

In the time it's taken me to come full circle, Ludo has crossed the road. He's standing in front of me, peering into my bag. "Have you got rum at home to go with all that Coke?"

I roll my eyes. "No, and it's not even mine. I buy it for the old dude above me. He doesn't get out much."

"And the cat food?"

"For the bat-fink that hangs around my garden."

"So you *do* think about people other than yourself?"

"I never said I didn't."

"Yes, you did."

"When?"

He shrugs. "I have no idea. Maybe you just thought it too loud, huh?"

When it comes to how my brain behaves around Ludo, I'll believe anything. And my silence seems to amuse him even more.

"You're definitely not the arsehole you think you are."

"I am."

Ludo steps away.

I panic and grab his arm. "Where are you going?"

"Home. You?"

I hold up my bag. "Same. Um . . . can I, uh, see you some time?"

"See me?"

"Yeah, like get a drink—a coffee or something?"

"Why?"

"Because I like spending time with you."

I can tell it's on the tip of Ludo's tongue to repeat his question, but he seems to catch himself and slowly nods.

"If you want. I can give you my number?"

He writes his phone number on my arm with a bright green Sharpie he digs out of his bag. His touch, as ever, nearly brings me to my knees, but I hold it together long enough to let him leave me again.

I watch him walk away, head bowed, tatty backpack slung over one shoulder. He moves like the world weighs him down, and I want to chase him across the road and ease his burden, but I'm in no state to chase anyone, and so I let him go and make my way home.

After delivering the bumper order of Coke to the old geezer upstairs, I retreat to the garden to feed the cat. He crawls out of the bushes and scarfs the food like it's been days since he last ate, not the few hours that have passed since I fed him this morning.

I don't actually know if the cat is male. It's an assumption I made a while ago, but I was drunk at the time, and I can't remember why. It's stuck anyway, and despite the fact the damn thing is a pest, I'm glad he survived my absence. Some days he's the only living soul I talk to. I used to relish that. I don't anymore.

The digits Ludo has scrawled on my skin tingle. I programme them into the shitty prepay phone Michael brought me and wonder why I didn't do it on the street. Why I didn't save Ludo the trouble of digging through his bag for a pen. Then I remember how it felt when he gripped my wrist and twisted my arm to suit him, and for once I thank my subconscious for doing me a favour.

I need a drink.

No, I don't. I haven't touched the stuff since Ludo rescued me from the slow death I was dying on the pavement opposite his house. It's been hard . . . too hard to back up my assertion that I'm not physically dependent on it, but at the same time, it's been easier than I deserve too. Truth is, I'm so fucking embarrassed that he saw me like that, on top of what he saw in the hospital, that my pride has kept me sober. How long that would've lasted if I hadn't run into him is anybody's guess.

My hands are still shaky. I alternate between sitting on them and clinging to my phone as though it's life raft in a drifting sea of apathy, staring at the blank screen. My cravings for a sweet hit of booze are at an all-time high, but they're eclipsed by something else, and with twitching thumbs, I unlock my phone and start typing.

Aidan: *hey*

I zoom—ha, limp—around my flat like a man possessed, tidying shit that doesn't need tidying, thankful that the sum total of my life belongings amount to little more than a small TV and the stack of magazines I brought home from the hospital. For reasons I'm yet to understand, I've invited Ludo over, and I'm so fucking nervous my head feels like it might explode at any moment.

Your place is a shithole.

But there's nothing more I can do about that, so I check the fridge for in-date milk and then collapse on my couch, clutching my phone, rereading our brief message exchange for the thousandth time.

Aidan: *hey*

Ludo: *Aidan?*

Aidan: *it's me. sorry. should've said.*

Ludo: *It's okay. I asked, so it's fine. Are you okay?*

Aidan: *yeah. are u?*

Ludo: *Yes. It was nice to see you.*

Aidan: *it was nice to see you too. I don't live far from where you saw me. do u want to come round some time?*

Ludo: *When?*

Aidan: *now?*

Ludo: *As in . . . right now?*

Aidan: *yeah, or as in, whenever ure free*

Ludo: *I have to walk my dog when the sun goes in. Maybe after?*

Aidan: *sounds good to me*

I've never been one for making plans, but as I sit in the fading daylight, waiting for Ludo to knock on my door, I regret not asking him for a rough time. The anticipation is killing me, and despite my housework binge knackering me, I can't sit still.

I get up and pace the small space that serves as my living room and my bedroom, imagining what I might say to him when he arrives or how I'll feel if he doesn't show up. My life up until this point is littered with broken promises and people I've let down. Is it karma if Ludo doesn't come? If he was humouring my text messages?

Why would he do that when he could've simply ignored you?

As has become my standard MO, I have no logical answer. Maybe—

A knock at the door startles me out of my fretting. I spin on my good leg and hurry to the hallway, all but ripping the door open. The pessimist in me half expects to find the milkman on the other side, even though I don't have a fucking milkman, but it's Ludo, in all his slender dark-eyed glory.

Despite my frantic pacing, I can't think of a single thing to say, so I stare at him while he shifts uncomfortably, until I remember how to be a functioning human being.

"Sorry. Come in."

Ludo hesitates, and it's all I can do not to grab him and tug him over the threshold, but I don't touch him . . . not yet. From day one we've been weirdly tactile—he laid his hands on me before we ever spoke—but there's something about him right now, an edginess I suspect has nothing to do with me and everything to do with him, so I let him be. I wait and eventually he comes inside.

I shut the door behind him. The urge to grab him is still there, but I ignore it and force myself to step around him and point to my shitty excuse for a kitchen. "I've got tea. Do you want some?"

Ludo bites his lip. His shoulders rise and fall too fast.

I give in and close my fingers around his scarred wrist. "It's dark and quiet in here, because that's how I like it, but we can sit in the garden if you like?"

"It's not that," Ludo whispers, and he finally meets my gaze. He clears his throat and takes a deep breath. "It's not that," he tries again. "It's, uh . . ."

He spins around in a slow circle, gesturing at my barren living space as though I should have a fucking clue what he's talking about.

I don't. But I know he's not happy, and that makes my chest ache. "What can I do to make it better?"

"Make what better?"

"Whatever's upsetting you."

Ludo sighs. "I'm not upset. I just got myself in a bit of a state rushing around to get to you, and now I'm here, I'm having a hard time dealing with the fact that this is where you live."

"It's shit, I know, but it's all I can afford."

I don't expect him to laugh. But he does, and it's so utterly humourless my toes curl, as though they can draw up into my body and avoid the bitterness lacing Ludo's rough bark of laughter.

"Aidan, it wouldn't bother me if you lived in a cave if it made you happy, but this?" He gestures around again. "This isn't home; it's a prison cell. *Look* at it."

I cross my arms over my chest. "I do look at it, every fucking day. What's so bad about it?"

"There's nothing here."

"What did you expect? Plush couches and plasma TVs in every room? All *two of them*. It's a bedsit, for Christ sakes."

"It's not—" Ludo starts, then he cuts himself off and turns to face me, guilt and regret marring his lovely face. "I'm not explaining myself properly. When I said there's nothing here, I mean there's nothing here that makes me think of you. Anyone could live here, and I don't like that. It reminds me of your hospital bed."

A glimpse of what he's trying to say creeps into my mind. I tighten my grip on his wrist and tug him forward. "Come with me."

He follows me into my living room—albeit, just my sofa bed and a small cabinet with a TV plonked on top of it. But in the cabinet is something that makes me think of my hospital bed too. I kneel on my good leg and retrieve the stack of magazines from where I stashed them earlier. There are so many of them that I can't get up without handing them to Ludo. "Here. I kept them all."

The first stirrings of a smile light up the shadows in Ludo's expression. He balances the magazines on one hand and helps me to my feet with the other. "I wasn't sure if you ever got them. I was a bit manic when all that happened, and I was worried I'd either imagined buying them or the nurses took them away before you woke up."

"I didn't know you were manic."

"Neither did I." He sits on the arm of the couch and leafs through the magazines. He comes to a cooking publication and holds it up. "But if I'd been thinking rationally, this might've clued me in. I take it you've never made the four-tier lemon cake on the front?"

I wince. Ludo smiles softly again, and the madman in me decides I'll make the fucking cake if it makes him happy. "I've never made the cake," I admit. "I'm not much of a cook if you don't fancy something on toast."

Ludo lowers the magazine and sets the rest of the stack aside, grin fading as though it was never there. "Bet you haven't got any bread."

"How did you know?"

"Because that's it." He springs like a cat to his feet and jabs a finger in my face. "*That's* what I'm talking about. You don't have anything here because you don't care enough about yourself to bother. I reckon your cupboards are bare, right? And there's sod all in your fridge?"

I can't deny. So I don't bother. I shrug and spread my hands. "I buy food when I need it."

"Do you have a duvet cover?"

"What?"

"A cover. On your duvet."

"I don't have a duvet."

"Sleeping bag?"

"Yup."

Ludo shakes his head so hard I half expect it to fly off. "I don't like that."

"Why?"

"I don't know."

His answer makes as much sense as this entire conversation, and it's not how I imagined his visit would go. But much of what I imagine about Ludo has little bearing on reality, so what the fuck can I do?

Ludo sighs and closes his eyes, and somehow I know he wishes he was closer to the wall so he could bang his head against it.

I reach for him again, grasping both his wrists this time and tugging him upright and closer to me. "Look, I'm sorry my place makes you uncomfortable. Before the accident I literally just slept here, so it didn't matter, and since . . . fuck, I don't know. I guess you're right, and I haven't cared enough to do anything about it."

"Do you think that will change?"

It's my turn to shrug. "I don't know."

Ludo mauls his bottom lip with his teeth. "I wish I could explain myself better—it's just that sometimes what happens in my head is nothing like what comes out of my mouth."

Hope sparks in my heart. "So you're not uncomfortable here?"

"No, it's not about me."

I don't understand, but I believe him. "We can still sit outside if you'd rather?"

Ludo shakes his head, gentler this time. "I'm hungry. Can we go to the shop?"

"Uh. Sure."

We leave my bedsit less than five minutes after he arrived. As we make the five-minute trip to the shop, I'm scared he won't come back with me. That he'll make me buy a multipack of Snickers bars, then piss off home.

In the shop Ludo buys sweet potatoes, red peppers, onions, and a small plastic tub of something I don't recognise. "I can only cook pasta," he says, apparently amused by my puzzled frown. "Maybe we can learn something new together."

The fear lifts from my chest, replaced by elation, and I don't know when my emotions became so extreme.

"Okay."

"You sure? We can get Super Noodles if you want? I'm sure we can both cook those."

"Yeah, but they're like tapeworms glued together, so—"

Ludo laughs again, for real this time, and I swear the sun twitches on its way to bed, like it wants to rise up again and get a better view of whoever made that fucking amazing sound. "Stop," he says. "Or I'll never be able to eat them again, and I like the chicken ones. They remind me of when being sick meant a day on the couch with a bottle of Lucozade."

"I remember those days too, but I didn't get Super Noodles." I point at the canned soup shelf. "I got Heinz cream of tomato straight out of the can with a fork to eat it with."

"That sounds messed up."

"That was my dad on a good day."

Ludo doesn't ask about my mum, and I don't pre-empt any questions with the fucked up information I'm happy to keep to myself. I grab a couple of packs of instant noodles and turn away. "Come on. Let's go, um, cook."

"You sure?"

"Of course I'm sure, mate. Let's learn something new . . . together, but take these just in case."

FIFTEEN

Ludo

Somehow, we fudge our way through Rita's magic soup recipe. Aidan has little interest in what goes in the pot, but he can handle a knife and I can't, and that's good enough for me.

We leave the vegetables to simmer with a healthy dash of the all-purpose seasoning I've stashed in Aidan's empty cupboards with the depleted bottle of sunflower oil. Maybe we'll go shopping again if I ever come back here.

"Come on," Aidan says. "Let's go outside."

Following him is easy, and he leads me onto a cute patio that's loaded with a wrought-iron bench and a bazillion plant pots. Flowers, herbs, there's even a young apple tree, and it's such a contrast from his soulless flat that I have to pinch myself to be sure my mind isn't turning yellow. "Wow. This is beautiful."

Aidan grunts and manoeuvres himself onto the bench, reminding me that he's been on his feet for the last two hours. "It's getting there. I lost some plants to frost when I was in hospital and then when I couldn't bend down, but most of them recovered."

"So I wasn't too far off when I bought you that copy of *Gardeners' World*?"

He treats me to a self-conscious chuckle. "I guess not. Don't ask me if I talk to them, though, cos I don't want to lie to you."

"You *do* talk to them."

"Shut up."

I purse my lips and crouch to examine his precious plants. He has a basil bush that's three times the size of the one I bought in the supermarket and about ten shades greener. I smell the perfumed leaves. "This is gorgeous."

"Have it," he says. "I don't do nothing with it."

"Not yet. I can teach you how . . . if you like?"

Aidan's eyes brighten enough for my heart to do a little jump. "Would you do that?"

"Of course. I like to cook, when I'm well, at least. It feels like healing, if that makes sense? Like . . . if I put good things in my body, it can only be good for my mind."

"It makes sense," Aidan says. "But I've always been fonder of the opposite. Abusing my body keeps my mind quiet."

"I get that."

The raised flesh on my arms burn. I rub them, and Aiden's gaze darkens with guilt.

"Sorry," he mutters.

"Why?"

"Because I'm an insensitive twat?"

"Who says you should be sensitive?"

"Everyone I've ever met."

"Well, they're wrong." I stand and wipe my sweaty palms on my jeans. "I don't need you to pretend my issues don't exist. It makes it too easy for me to do the same."

"It doesn't make it better when you can forget about it a while?"

His expression is as open as I've ever seen it. I claim the space next to him on the bench and draw a circle on the back of his hand. "You'd think, but no. All that does is make me crash harder when reality bites. I have to accept what bipolar means for me, even the shit bits."

"There's good bits?"

I laugh. Can't help it. "Sometimes. Did I ever tell you my favourite colour is yellow?"

He gets it straight away. Of course he does, and I wonder how many times I've told him that before. If I wittered on about it at his bedside when I was manic in the hospital.

Aidan reaches behind him and plucks a tiny yellow flower from a nearby pot, then reaches for another, blue this time. He presses both into my hand but doesn't speak, and I'm learning that to hear him the loudest, he doesn't have to.

Aidan doesn't have a blender, so we pulverise the soup with a handheld drill he's never used. The vegetables are super soft because we forgot about them simmering on the stove, and they disintegrate perfectly. Maybe it was meant to happen.

I take the pan off the stove while Aidan removes the drill bit and rinses it under the tap. "Is the drill broken now?"

"Wouldn't matter if it was. It's been in a box for two years."

"Is that how long you've lived here?"

"No. I've been here three years."

I'm horrified that he's been going to bed with a sleeping bag for three years, but I bite my tongue. I've given him enough earache about his home to last a lifetime. Besides, my house is chaos. Who the hell am I to judge him for keeping things simple?

Simple. Right. It's a word I often apply to Aidan, and it's a misnomer really, because he's dark and complex, and nothing about him is plain to see. Like now, when he takes the pan from me and peers at the contents—I can't tell if he didn't want me to carry something heavy or if he's curious about what we've made.

Maybe it's both.

Regardless, he doesn't have a ladle either, so he pours our dinner into cereal bowls and hands me a teaspoon to eat with. "Sorry, I don't eat much soup."

"You should. It's cheap and good for you."

"Cheaper than noodles?"

"Overall, yes. You could make four meals for fifty pence."

"Uh-huh." He limps to his couch and sits down.

I trail after him and drop beside him. "Try it. I bet it's nice."

He dips his spoon into the thick, spicy soup. "It smells nice. I don't think I've ever eaten anything this orange that wasn't radioactive."

"Radioactive?"

"Wotsits," he clarifies. "Nothing that orange that isn't a fruit or vegetable can be anything else."

"Sage advice."

He answers me by sliding his spoon into his mouth, and I'm instantly distracted by how full his lips are. He's insanely sexy, and I fight to keep my attraction to him in check. Aidan and I share something I've never felt with anyone else. I can't let the fact that I want to kiss him ruin it. *I* can't ruin it.

"Hey."

I jump as Aidan's hand lands on my shoulder. "Huh? What?"

"You spaced," he says, and I can tell he's trying not to stare at me. "Are you okay?"

"Yeah."

I don't explain, and he doesn't ask me to. His hand slips from my shoulder and he carries on eating his soup, his face lighting up with genuine pleasure the further down his bowl he gets.

Unable to resist, I dive in too, and I'm instantly rewarded by the magic Rita promised coating my tongue. The soup is sunshine and warmth, and we made it together. I'm sure that makes it taste even better.

We empty our bowls in two minutes flat. Aidan rises to refill us, but I tug him down and go instead. When we're full, I put the leftovers in the fridge and return to the couch. It's probably time for me to go home, but I don't want to. Not yet. I don't want to leave the tiny bedsit I suddenly feel safe in, and I don't want to leave Aidan.

You see, two bowls of soup aren't enough, and it never will be. Aidan needs more from me and from himself.

I crouch in front of him and place my hands on his knees. I'm unsure of what I need to say, and so I don't say anything. And neither does he, at least, not with words. He leans forwards and takes a breath.

And then he kisses me.

SIXTEEN

Aidan

I didn't mean to kiss him, but even if he pushes me away, I know I'll never regret it.

But he doesn't push me away. He snatches a sharp, startled breath, and then he kisses me back, soft and sweet, like the rustle of leaves at the very top of my favourite tree. I sense the smile on his lips, and it warms what space I have left in my bitter heart that he hasn't already filled.

I wonder if he's humouring me. Then his hands slide up my thighs, and he clasps my face, tugging me closer. The intensity of our kiss ramps up a gear. My head swims, but I don't dare clutch at him to steady myself. I don't dare *move* in case I break this spell.

A lifetime seems to pass as his lips move with mine, but at the same time, however long we're pressed together is over in a flash.

Ludo pulls away, his face twisted in an expression so sheepish and rueful that I have to fight with myself in case I spring from the couch and tackle him to the floor. God, I want him. And damn, if I don't care about him so fucking much that if the next words out of his mouth are that this was a mistake, I can live with it. I *will* live with it. Anything to be close to him for a little while longer.

A breathless laugh escapes him. "Sorry," he says. "I didn't mean to jump on you."

"I started it."

"True." He licks his reddened lips, and his gaze slips to my mouth.

Kiss me again. Please.

But he doesn't. He stands and shakes his head. "I should go."

"I don't want you to."

"I know, but I still should. That way I can come back another time."

I don't understand what could possibly happen if he stayed to prevent him coming back, and I don't need to. The fact that he *wants* to come back is everything. Bracing myself on the arm of the couch, I stand too. Our faces are inches apart, but I force myself not to kiss him again and walk him to the door.

Ludo opens it and takes a step outside. Then he turns back, eyes wide. "You know why I'm leaving, don't you? It isn't because I don't want to stay."

"I know."

"Are you sure? Because I haven't explained."

"You don't have to. I know what would happen if you stayed . . . at least, I know how it pans out in *my* head."

I regret the words as soon as they're out of my mouth, but Ludo's nervous smile morphs into a wicked, dirty grin, and I remember that he's a grown man who is so much more than the illness that puts such fear in his eyes. My body floods with heat, but I dampen it down and lean on the doorframe. "Seriously," I say. "I get it. Just don't leave it too long before you come back."

Ludo leans in and kisses my cheek. "I won't."

"You want me to do admin work?" I glare at Bernard, horror seeping through me as I picture the porta-cabin he calls an office and the gaggle of women who work there.

"I need it doing and you need a job to keep you going before you're back up them trees. Sounds like a fair deal to me."

He shrugs as though it's a done deal, and he's right: it's more than a fair deal considering he's been paying me for sod all since the accident.

I still want to punch him in the face, though, and it takes all my favourite Ludo memories to stop me doing it.

Bernard buys me another cup of tea, then leaves me to it in the greasy spoon café he invited me to for a "business breakfast." With him gone, I sit back in my chair, relieved. Despite my aversion to working in his office, I've been shitting myself that he was going to ditch me all week. The fact that he hasn't, *and* that he seems to believe I'll be fit enough one day to do my old job, has left me feeling ten stone lighter.

I sip my tea while I scroll through my phone. It's been three days since I last spoke to Ludo and a week since he came over and taught me to make soup. My lips pulse and throb as I recall every second they spent pressed against his, but I don't text him. It's his turn to message me, and so far I've made myself stick to that rule. Ludo is unlike anyone I've ever known, but instinct tells me to give him space. That if he wants to talk to me, to see me, to kiss me again, he will. For now, that he answers my sporadic messages is enough.

As if on cue, my phone flashes. I grip it tighter, but the message that invades my screen isn't Ludo; it's Michael, and my mood drops like a stone. My usual MO is to ignore him, but for reasons I can't comprehend, I open the message.

Michael: *Just wondering how you are. We're having a BBQ next week and would love you to come. No drinking, though, okay?*

Only Michael could express concern for me, make me feel wanted, and judge the shit out of me in one message. I want to delete it and pretend it never arrived, but I know that will only lead to phone calls I'll have to ignore too. Knocks at the door. Notes through my letterbox. *Fuck that shit.* There's only one person I want knocking at my door, and it's the only soul on earth who's never judged me. I picture Ludo's sweet face as I tap out words I don't mean to my cousin.

Aidan: *might be working, i'll let you know. thanks for asking me though, would love to see u too*

Michael doesn't reply, leaving me to believe that perhaps he didn't mean it either, but as I toss my phone on the table, it lights up again. And it's Ludo.

Huh. Maybe karma is a thing.

Ludo

I meet Aidan in the woods. Somehow it seems safer than my house or his, for him at least, if the dreams I've been having about him are anything to go by. In the back of my mind, I'm grateful that my obsession with him is allowing me to sleep better than I have in months, but still. Aidan lit a fire with his kiss, and I'm having trouble keeping it under control.

He's waiting for me by the tree I've come to think of as his. It's a long way from his bedsit, and when he's slow to rise from his perch on a nearby stump, I worry that I've made him walk too far.

"It's fine." He dismisses my concern with a wave of his work-hardened hands. "Does me good to get out, especially if I don't go to the pub."

"Which pub do you go to?"

"None if I can help it, but that's a recent thing. I used to spend every night in the Red Lion."

"Sounds fun."

"It really wasn't."

"Then why did you do it?"

He shrugs and swings his gaze with Bella as she darts after a squirrel. "Habit. I grew up in pubs, keeping my old man company. I feel at home in them, so it's hard to stay away when I don't feel at home anywhere else."

It makes sense, considering the sterile nature of his bedsit. I can't fault him for cleanliness, especially from a man who claims not to care about anything, but then, there's nothing in Aidan's home to get cluttered or dirty. "Did you finish the soup?"

Aidan's eyebrow twitches, as though the banality of my question amuses him. "Of course I did. I ate it for breakfast, lunch, and dinner until it was all gone."

A laugh bursts out of me, and the awkward cloud hanging over us dissipates. Bella returns from squirrel hunting with a stick in her mouth. She presents it to Aidan. He tosses it into the wilderness, and we follow as she crashes after it.

We hike in silence for a while. With Aidan by my side, the vast forest seems less daunting, and it's . . . nice. Despite his spiky personality, his predilection for gruff quiet has always comforted me, a stark contrast to the noise and chaos I often need to feel calm.

I don't know what he's thinking, though, if he's enjoying the sun-dappled tranquillity as much as I am. As ever, he's impossible to read, so I don't try and, instead, turn to recalling a million different things about his beautiful lips. How they press into a thin line when he's in pain, the snarl he pulls when he's annoyed, and how wonderful they felt when he pressed them against mine.

It's been years since a boy kissed me. My last serious relationship was with the most beautiful girl in the world, but she never kissed me like Aidan did. She was made of glass—too precious to touch—and I scared her away.

Aidan isn't scared of me, perhaps because he doesn't understand how destructive I can be, to my own life and anyone unlucky enough to get close to me, but none of that mattered when he kissed me. His lips made me feel like his most treasured thing, and I want, more than anything, for him to kiss me again.

We reach a clearing with a circle of fallen trees, each with patterns carved into the trunks. I've always found them bewitching, but what about Aidan? Trees are his life's work, his passion. There is nothing that lights his face more. "Do you think they're defaced?"

"Hmm?"

"The trees. I like them, but I sometimes wonder if they should've been left in their natural state."

Aidan sits on one of the trees in question. He stretches his legs out in front of him and massages his thigh. I want to do it for him, but I don't know how, so whether he'd want me to or not seems irrelevant. "They're not defaced," he says after a while. "But I'd flip my shit if I saw someone doing it to a healthy tree."

I believe him, and I don't want to think too hard about what he means by *flip my shit*. Even with his bum leg, Aidan is built for scrapping. "We can go back, you know . . . if you've had enough walking."

"Go back where?"

"My house."

Something indecipherable flickers in his dark gaze. "I wasn't sure you'd want me to come over again."

"Why not?"

"Because you don't like people in your house, and I pounced on you when you came to mine."

So we are talking about it. The anxiety-ridden monster in me kind of hoped we could pretend the kiss never happened and is permanently at war with the rest of me that wants to do it over and over again. "I told you already that you're different, and I really didn't mind when you pounced on me."

"You didn't?"

"No." It pains me that he'd think so, but I can't find the words, so I twist on the fallen tree and grab the hand that's not rubbing his thigh. I bring his fingers to my lips and kiss them gently. "But I'm not very good at having normal relationships, so I don't know what to do with it."

"Normal relationships." Aidan echoes me with a bemused expression. "The fuck even are they?"

For the second time today, I laugh without care, and it feels so good that for a moment, I can't stop. "I don't know," I say when I've composed myself. "Does it matter?"

"Not to me. I couldn't give a shit what's normal, mate."

I like it when he calls me *mate*. It makes me think of wolves and foxes and swans and an entirely different kind of mate to what he probably means. It's primal and *so fucking normal* in a way most humans don't think anymore. "I want to kiss you again. Like, properly, you know? Without one of us leaving."

Aidan makes a sound low in his throat. "I could get on board with that."

A white-hot thrill licks through my body. It scares and excites me in equal measure and I make no move to put my money where my mouth desperately wants to go.

"I got a new job," Aidan blurts.

I blink and realise I'm still clutching his hand. "Wow. That's awesome."

"It ain't. Bernard wants me to work in his office with his missus and sister-in-law. You better kiss me quick cos I might not make it through Monday."

I can't tell if he's using humour to deflect from something he can see in my face. My mum once told me the whole world knew I was a mess before I did. I squeeze Aidan's fingers and try and picture him in the office. I can't do that either.

Aidan shifts on his log. "Look," he says quietly. "Just because we want to do things doesn't mean we have to do them any time soon. I'm good with hanging out, and if you want to kiss me again . . . well, fuck, I'm not gonna stop you."

"I want to."

"I know."

I take a deep breath, letting it rattle through my ribs and into my limbs. In my head, I kiss him now, and it's the perfect footnote to a fairy tale I don't quite understand.

Back in the real world, I stand and tug on his hand. "Let's go to the shop."

Aidan

"Do you like meatballs?"

I glance up from the rosemary bush I'm planting at the bottom of his overgrown garden. I've cleared most of the dead shrubs away already, and the herb patch he wants will be awesome if I can get it done before the summer heat fades. "How are you going to make meatballs when all you bought was sausages and an onion?"

"Sausages are meat. I'm going to roll them up like my nonna used to."

He disappears back into the house. I watch him go, transfixed by the elegant sway of his body. He's put on a bit of weight since we met in the hospital, his limbs no longer delicate. They are capable, and I want him to come and dig in the earth with me.

I want a lot of things, but I settle for continuing my quest to give him a garden that excites him. You see, Ludo is going to make my home more like his, and I'm going to make his garden more like mine. In between, I'm trying not to touch him too much or stare at him too long, because I don't want to scare him.

It scares *me* how much I want to kiss him. How I dream about it when we're not together, more than anything else that keeps me from a peaceful sleep. Kissing has never meant much to me. Scratch that. Before him it's never meant *anything*, and waiting for him to break the stalemate between us is killing me.

Not that I can complain about spending the last four days on the trot with him. We have a routine. A morning walk in the woods, a trip to the shop, then he either cooks enough food to load my fridge-freezer for a month or leads me to his house where he cooks enough for just the two of us while I destroy his garden enough to rebuild it.

No kissing.

Absolutely no kissing.

Ludo comes outside again. He crouches by my side, frowning. "I have to work tomorrow."

My heart sinks, but I've been expecting this, the pinprick in the bubble around us. "You never told me what you do for work."

"It's not very interesting."

"I'm interested." I keep my gaze on the sandy soil—I've learnt that Ludo doesn't like me looking too closely when he's talking about himself. "In fact, I went to bed last night thinking about it. I'm thinking you're probably, like, a web designer or some shit. You're creative, right?"

Ludo snorts, and it's so derisive I drop my trowel. "I'm not creative." Bitterness laces his tone. "I'm chaotic. Don't confuse the two."

I open my mouth to speak, but he cuts me off with a minute shake of his head.

"I *am* chaotic, and it's where the colour in my life comes from—yellow and black remember? So I need a beige and grey job to keep me grounded. It would be mayhem otherwise."

It takes me a moment to decipher his code, and even then, it's far from an exact translation. "Are you saying you have to do a boring job because you can't handle anything that excites you?"

"Something like that." He sits back on his heels. "And don't start asking me what my hopes and dreams were when I was a kid, because I didn't have any."

"Ludo—"

"*Aidan.*"

There's a warning in the way he says my name, but the horse has bolted, leaving the stable door swinging in the wind. "There must've been something you wanted to do."

"There really wasn't. I spent my childhood watching my cousin dance like a fucking swan and my teenage years wishing life stayed that simple."

I flinch. Can't help it. I've got a mouth like a drunk sailor, but Ludo is cleverer than me and uses words that mean something. I can count on one hand the occasions I've heard him swear. "So what *do* you do for work?"

"Software testing. It's nothing like what you do, but it gives me structure when I'm struggling to focus, and I can duck out when I need to. It suits me."

I disagree, but what the fuck do I know? Despite another round of late night googling I've done, Ludo's illness remains a mystery to me, and it's absolutely not my place to have an opinion on how he lives his life. "Working on the trees made me as happy as I let myself be. I wish you had that too."

He grunts again, and I can't fucking deal with it. I get to my feet like I'm eighty-five years old and limp inside to use the bog.

Ludo's bathroom doesn't make me feel any better. It's spotlessly clean and by far the only tidy room in the house, but it's still a riot of colour. Yellow walls, a pink suite from the seventies, topped off with zebra print towels. Chaotic or not, it's still *him*. It doesn't seem fair that he can't be like this all the time. That the brightness in him that's so addictive to me could do him any harm.

He's waiting for me on the half landing of his curved staircase, anxiety rolling off him in jagged waves of tension. "You don't understand."

I sit on the top step. "Do I need to?"

"I don't know."

Measuring words has never come easily to me. Before Ludo I've rarely tried, but I make a valiant attempt now. "Look, I don't care what you do for a living, and I never even said you should be doing something else. I think maybe . . . uh, you've had this conversation with other people and they didn't let you speak?"

Ludo tilts his head sideways. Sitting on the carpet that's the only beige thing about him, knees hugged to his chest, he seems so young that I have to revisit his lips on mine to remember he's a fucking adult.

And then, of course, my ability to think clearly is pretty much obliterated. I swear, having girlfriends in school when all I wanted was to snog the captain of the football team was way easier than this.

"You're right," Ludo says eventually. "No one listens to me. I mean, Rita does, but she's paid to, and even she doesn't really take me seriously."

"The soup woman?"

"Yeah." Ludo laughs. "She's my CPN."

"Huh?"

"Community psychiatric nurse. My babysitter, basically, though it's probably down to her that I don't get sectioned much any more."

Disquiet flares in my gut. "When did you last get sectioned?"

"A few years ago. I stopped taking my medication and I thought I could fly. I get delusional, see, if my manic episodes go on too long."

"And then you come down? Like . . . uh, crash? Is that the right word?"

Ludo shrugs. "It works. And yeah, what goes up always has to come down, and sometimes it's so fast no one can catch me, not even myself. But I'm getting better at recognising when I need help, so I'm hoping it won't happen again, at least, not that badly."

I think about what he said in hospital about falling a lot and the gruesome list of injuries he listed as though they meant nothing. Are they connected? If they are, I shudder to think how, but this is as open as Ludo has ever been about his bipolar, and I need to learn as much as I can for as long as he's willing to talk. "What medication do you take?"

"Lithium to stabilise my moods, and an anti-depressant. I used to take an anti-psychotic too, but it didn't work like it had on other people."

The masochist in me is curious, and I can't help raising a questioning eyebrow.

"It made my delusions normal," Ludo says. "Like, I'd still have them, but I'd be less bothered by them, which actually made them more dangerous. If I'm frightened, I don't come out of my house."

I swallow hard. The fact that he has to be frightened to feel safe is so fucking unfair that I want to punch a hole in his funky coloured walls. My knuckles contract. Fingernails dig into my palm, and I grit my teeth.

"It's not always like that, though," Ludo continues when I don't speak. "Sometimes I'm not scared of anything regardless of what meds I'm on, and that's magic. It's what makes me not resent being bipolar . . . the perfect balance of mania and reality. It doesn't happen often, but it's pretty fucking special."

"Stop swearing. You're freaking me out."

"Sorry."

I shake my head. "That's not what I meant."

"What did you mean then?"

"That it doesn't seem like my perception of you when you speak in a way I'm not used to."

Ludo snorts. "That sentence doesn't sound like *you*."

He has a point, but being around him has broadened my vocabulary. What can I say? Wordsmith, innit? "Whatever. I need to get that rosemary in the ground before it dries out. Are we cool?"

"Aidan, I've never been cool."

I don't agree with that either, but I bite my tongue as I tug him to his feet and follow him downstairs. Talking isn't my bag at the best of times, and I've said enough for one day.

Later, I wash our dinner pots and pans and put them away. Then I rinse the plates and stack them in the dishwasher. Ludo, pissed off because I won't let him wait on me, has disappeared.

It takes me a while to find him, mainly because my knee, sore from a day in the garden, can't handle the stairs at a pace faster than a slow death.

I ease myself onto the landing and glance around. His bedroom door is closed and he's not in the bathroom, so I poke my head round the door to the spare room. It's small, just big enough for a two-seater couch and some shelves and, unlike the rest of the house, is plainly decorated. Ludo is curled up with a book clutched to his chest, completely and wonderfully asleep.

The sight of him takes my breath away. I've watched him sleep a dozen times, but it was different in the hospital. That place was a hellhole. Here, while I know he has good food in his belly and no surgeon's stitches holding him together, a quiet peace steals over me.

He's resting, and he's beautiful.

Ignoring the searing protest in my knee, I kneel and push silky dark hair back from Ludo's face for no other reason than I want to. My lips burn with the desire to kiss him goodbye, but I swallow it and squeeze his hand instead.

He doesn't stir. I find a scrap of paper and a pencil. My handwriting is shite, but I persevere and scrawl him a note. Then, with a yearning in my heart that fucking drowns me, I lock his house up and leave him.

SEVENTEEN

Ludo

"What if I become dependent on him? What if I already am?"

Rita watches me as I pace her office. There are no biscuits on her desk this time, no cake wrapped in paper for me. Because this isn't my regular appointment. This is me invading her day and disrupting her hard-earned lunch break. "Being friends with someone doesn't make you dependent on them."

"Yes, it does."

"No, Ludo, it really doesn't. I have lots of friends I miss when they're not around. It just means I love them."

I stop pacing and wheel around. "I don't love Aidan."

"I never said you did. I'm talking about how I feel about my friends and how it's probably not that different to how you feel about yours."

"I don't have any friends."

"Aidan is your friend. You do nice things for each other, and you enjoy spending time together."

Aidan is my friend. Aidan is my friend. Aidan is my friend.

But even as I repeat it over and over, it doesn't feel right.

Nothing has, ever since I woke up to a dark spare room, screaming into an empty house because Aidan left.

You had a bad dream, like you always do in that room. It had nothing to do with the fact that Aidan did what any normal person would do when their host fell asleep—he went home.

My long-maligned rational side knows this. How can I not when Aidan *texted me to tell me*? But the anxiety I woke with has dug its claws in, and now real, deep-rooted, and yet totally unfounded fear is threatening the first new friendship I've made in this godforsaken town.

Stop it. You like Buckbourne.

But do I? I moved here because London scared me, and it was far enough away from anyone I knew that I didn't have to live with the fact that *I* scared *them*, but that doesn't make it home. Nothing felt like home until Aidan.

"Ludo." Rita sounds distant even as she stands and comes to where I've ground to a halt by the window. "I have ten minutes before my next patient. If we're going to get anywhere, you need to talk to *me*, not yourself."

I turn to her. "It's myself talking to myself about myself."

"I know, but maybe we should try speaking out loud for the time we have left. Then I'll give you a new notebook to take home."

Super.

I leave Rita's clinic with two new notebooks and a prescription for a single Valium dose. The pharmacy is on my way home. I consider walking on by, but three days of peak ridiculous is taking its toll. I need to eat and sleep and sensibly think my way out of this mess before it turns into something I can't fix.

Back home, common sense tells me to wait until tonight before I take the sedative. That sleeping all day will only lead to the kind of night I fear most—sleepless and afraid. But I'm so done with the noise in my head that I can't fight temptation.

I swallow the magic pill and go to bed.

I wake to the darkness I don't want to face. Mouth dry, I crawl out of bed and stumble downstairs. I gulp water and scour the fridge as my stomach grumbles to life. Finally I'm hungry. Famished, in fact, and I eat everything edible left in the fridge while leaning against the kitchen counter.

When I'm full, I take Bella for a quick spin around the block, then feed her too, guilt at neglecting her all day nibbling the edges of my sedative haze. I walked her for miles before visiting Rita—I had to, to avoid Aidan's precious tree—and I know she was perfectly content to share my bed with me, but she's the happiest dog in the world. She doesn't deserve my silence.

We play ball in the garden. Somehow she knows to be careful of the herb patch Aidan hasn't yet finished.

I can't look at it, but in the cool air of the late evening, my thoughts have finally slowed enough for me to catch up with them. Rita's notebooks are on the kitchen counter next to the empty blister pack the Valium came in. I clear the rubbish away and take a notebook to the couch. Challenging my negative thoughts is a way of life for me. CBT, talking therapies, I've done them all, and they work when I have the wherewithal to let them.

Chewing my lip, I retrace my steps to Sunday, when I last saw Aidan. He was standing at my kitchen sink, washing up, whistling through his teeth despite the fact that I preceded dinner with a mini meltdown over something he hadn't even said. Yeah, he was right about that. People don't listen to me, so I spoke without giving him the chance to try.

Idiot.

No.

I'm not an idiot. I'm living with a mental illness. Sometimes I fuck up.

I write it down and then cross out the F-bomb. Aidan is right about that too.

It takes me an hour to piece together the anxiety trail. An unscheduled nap, a bad dream, failure to catch my negative thoughts before they spun me into a vicious cycle of fear and self-loathing. It's a pattern I've drawn a thousand times, and I ponder if I'll ever stop.

Still. The Valium and my full stomach have thrown up a roadblock. For the first time in days, I can think clearly. I find my phone and scroll through the messages Aidan has sent me over the last few days and my sporadic replies.

Aidan: *snuck out while you were sleeping. speak tomorrow*

Aidan: *morning. going to work in a bit. call u later?*

Aidan: *hope ur ok*

Ludo: *I'm fine.*

Aidan: *um, good? u wanna walk after work?*

Aidan: *sure ur okay?*

Aidan: *hello?*

Ludo: *I'm fine*

Aidan: *okay. bell me whenever u want*

Wow. If anyone has the right to be insecure, it's not me. But I can't help how terrified I am that Aidan's concern for me makes me feel good. Makes me feel valid and wanted, but at the same time so unworthy I want to take his messages and set them on fire. He doesn't deserve to care about me. It will only hurt him and then hurt me when he can't take it anymore.

"Ludovico, leave your cousin alone. He doesn't have time for your silly games."

My aunt pulls Angelo away from me and out of the room. I scream as he goes, and I scream and scream until my mum comes in and shuts me up. "He's not yours. Now be quiet, your father's embarrassed of you."

I blink away my ten-year-old cousin's lovely face, it's perfection marred by confusion. One day I'll get over the fact that I never saw him again, but today isn't that day, and I have other things—other perfect faces—on my mind. I read through Aidan's messages one more time; then I delete them and shove my phone in a drawer. I was an impossible child, and now I'm a difficult man. Aidan doesn't need that in his life—no one does.

The rest of my evening passes in a haze of catching up on work and tidying away the mess I've somehow created by doing nothing at all. My phone calls to me every time I come in the kitchen, but I ignore it. It's been twenty-four hours since Aidan last messaged me, and I'm so sure he's done that I'm almost relieved. Without him I can get back to the monotony I need to stay sane—the beige that keeps me safe. Maybe I'll paint the rest of the house the same puke-esque cream as the spare room—

My phone rings. I freeze, my hand on the kettle. It could be anyone, but of course it's Aidan, unless I worried Rita enough for her to check up on me.

Such a thing isn't unheard of, but I know it's Aidan, and the drawer is *right next to me*. My hand twitches. I ball it into a fist but reach for the drawer with the other before I can stop myself.

My battered iPhone greets me, lit up with Aidan's name and the photo of the rosemary bush I've assigned to his contact.

I should've blocked his number.

But I didn't because I don't want to. I want—no, *need*—to hear his voice, even if it's for the last time.

I take the call. "Hey."

"Hey yourself." His voice is scratchy and rough, as though he's been smoking a lot. "Am I disturbing you? Fuck, I didn't realise how late it is."

I glance at the clock and roll my eyes. "It's nine o'clock."

Aidan yawns. "That's late for me when I'm working. Getting up early basically turns me into my dad."

Shut it down. Shut it down. Shut it down. "Your dad? What's he like?"

"Dead. And probably just as well. He was a nasty bastard."

It makes sense. Aidan is all sharp edges and deflective defence. He's not a man who's been loved. "When did he die?"

"A few years ago. I don't count them anymore."

"Because you hated him?"

"No, because I didn't care enough even for that."

That wounds me. It shouldn't, but it does. I don't want Aidan to be a man who doesn't care about anything. Who walks through life cold and believing himself unlovable. He is kind and funny and gorgeous, and God, I wish he knew it.

So tell him.

My brain does a one-eighty. Suddenly pushing him away doesn't seem so important. I pour water from the kettle into a mug already loaded with lavender tea. It tastes like soap, but Rita told me purple and blue are calming colours, and I need all the purple right now. "What about your mum?"

"She's dead too."

"When?"

"A long time ago."

He doesn't want to talk about that—about any of it. But he wants to talk or he wouldn't have called. And clearly I want to talk or I wouldn't have answered the damn phone.

I take my mug upstairs to my bedroom. The spare room door is closed, like it has been since I stumbled out of there three nights ago. I open it now and peer inside at the drab walls. It's not a space that makes me think of Aidan, and I feel bad that he had to come in here to find me.

"Ludo?"

"Yeah?"

"Nothing. Was checking you were there. You haven't said anything for, like, an hour."

I laugh, slopping tea over my hand. "An hour? Okay. For your information, I was just coming upstairs to settle down so I can talk to you properly."

"Properly, eh? Does that involve ignoring my messages for days at a time? Cos, mate, it'd be easier if you told me to fuck off."

And there it is: the brutality of him that I find so refreshing. He didn't press me in his messages because that's not who he is. He does things right or he doesn't do them at all, even if it means things go wrong. "I'd never tell you to fuck off."

"Well, you can if you ever need to, so don't be worrying about hurting my feelings or some shit if you need some space."

I feel like we had this conversation before, but I can't remember when or how. Déjà vu often haunts me. Keeps me awake at night. Taints my days with doubt. But I like it with Aidan. It's as if there's whole parts of our friendship that might come back to me later. Like shoring up my stash of him for a rainy day. "I don't need space—"

But that's not true. A Valium and a top up dose of him hasn't changed the fact that I'm frightened of how much I like him. "I'm sorry," I say instead.

"It's okay," he says. "You don't owe me your time. I was just worried in case you needed me and I didn't know."

I start to say that I don't need him, that I can't need anyone *ever*. But that's a lie too. Because I do need him—I needed *this*, a quiet conversation that doesn't have to make sense. "Sometimes . . . sometimes I get a bit lost in my own head. I'm scared of the things I like in case I lose them."

"Uh-huh. I get that, and I'm not going to promise the worst shit in the world won't ever happen, but . . . fuck, I don't know. I'm scared too, Ludo. I'm scared I'll say the wrong thing and upset you more. I'm scared I'll squeeze you so hard I'll break you."

"Do you mean literally?"

"I don't think so. I think for the first time in my life I might've understood how a sentence doesn't have to be, uh, literal to mean something."

I curl up on my bed, clutching my phone to my ear hard enough to leave a dent in my face. Warmth spreads through me, and I wish he were here so I could smooth the frown lines from his face. "I'm sorry I ignored you. I didn't want to, I just—I lost my head a bit."

"Did you find it yet?"

"I think so. My CPN gave me a Valium."

Aidan hums, deep and low like a gathering storm. "I could do with one of those after three days in Bernard's office. Those women are bananas."

I've forgotten that he's started a new job he was sure he'd hate. More guilt bites me, but knowing he's right there tempers it. I can say sorry for that when I see him. When I sit him down and feed him the biggest dinner ever and prod him into sharing everything I've missed.

We talk some more, but eventually Aidan calls time. "I get to leave the office tomorrow," he says, and I can tell how much it excites him. "Bernard is letting me assess a tree and write up a plan for dealing with it."

"Is that worse than not working outside at all?"

"I'll tell you tomorrow."

"Yeah?"

"Yeah. Listen, I'm gonna go to the shop on my way home, then have a bash at making something that doesn't look like road kill. If you're hungry, come over. If you're not, I'll speak to you soon, okay?"

There are so many things I want to say, but I nod, even though he can't see me. "Okay."

And then he's gone. A quiet click takes him away from me, but the lost sensation I've carried for days is no longer there. I can see Aidan tomorrow. For real.

I close my eyes. Excitement buzzes in my veins, eclipsing the disturbance of the last few days, and somehow, despite the fact that I've lost a whole day to a Valium coma, I fall asleep.

EIGHTEEN

Aidan

I don't know if Ludo will show up. And if he does, I have zero clue what we're going to do. Common sense dictates that we'll slide into the routine we've followed for weeks now, but a nagging in my heart tells me something between us has changed. And it has nothing to do with kissing.

Or not kissing.

Whatever.

It's definitely my turn to cook.

After work I refuse Bernard's offer of a pint and schlep to the shop nearest my place. It's not as posh as the one Ludo uses. It caters to the handful of flats and bedsits rather than the bazillion listed cottages and mansions, but it's got sausages—which I *know* Ludo likes—and frozen chips. Even I can't fuck that up, right?

I'm starving, but I walk home vowing not to cook until Ludo arrives. Relief almost drowns me when I find him waiting on my doorstep. "All right, mate?"

He throws me a tired smile. "I am now. What did you get?"

"Bangers." I hold my shopping bag up. "And chips. That okay?"

"Anything that isn't hospital food is okay with me."

I feel bad that I haven't cooked for him before, but it's hard to do something I know I'm shit at when he does it so much better. And he's comfortable in the kitchen—his or mine. Relaxed. Happy. I'm addicted to watching him when he thinks I'm busy in the garden. The way he bites his lip when he's peering into the pasta pot, messy hair in his eyes. I try not to think about the fact that he won't touch a knife. To wonder *why* when the reality is I already know, even if he hasn't told me.

He might never tell me.

"Aidan?"

"Yeah?"

Ludo bites his bottom lip. "I'm sorry I've been a weirdo."

"You're not a weirdo."

"Not true."

"It is if you're apologising for having mental health issues, mate. Fuck that noise." I turn my back on him and open the door. It swings shut behind me, but Ludo catches it with his foot and follows me inside.

He doesn't speak for ages, so I busy myself turning the oven on and searching for the baking trays he bought me a few weeks ago. It takes me far too long to remember that loaded silences freak him out.

It helps that I'm kind of stuck in a misguided crouch. I hold out my hand. "Can you help me up?"

Ludo comes to life in ways I can't describe. He takes my outstretched hand and pries the other from the counter. I borrow his strength and balance as he hauls me to my feet, and somehow we end up nose-to-nose. In the murky depths of my mind I consider breaking every vow I've made about kissing him, but I don't move. I don't breathe.

I just stare at him and pray that one day soon, *he'll* kiss *me*.

As though he can hear my thoughts, Ludo licks his lips, and I trace his tongue as it darts out in its fleeting sweep. I have never wanted someone so bad in my whole life. I'm hot. I'm cold. I'm shaking, and yet I'm frozen in place. Only my heart seems to move freely, and every thudding beat is for him.

Ludo squeezes his eyes shut. "I know I keep trying to explain inexplicable things, but you have to know how good you make me feel when you look at me like that."

"Why are you closing your eyes then?"

"Because it scares me, Aidan. Everything does. Do you know how it feels to never be sure if you're truly happy or sliding into mania? To distrust every emotion?"

Of course I don't. I don't have the first clue what it's like to be Ludo, but I want to. I want to know everything he's prepared to tell me.

Fuck it. I take a chance and press a soft kiss to his glorious cheekbone. "I don't know how you feel, but I know how *I* feel, and that scares me a bit too."

"Why?"

"Because it's brand new. I'm not used to liking people."

Ludo snorts and opens his eyes. "You're pretty likeable too, you know."

"Uh-huh. Do you want bread and butter with your dinner?"

The standoff is over, and for once it's a clean break. Ludo nods and releases his death grip on my hands. "For sure. I'll do it."

It's on the tip of my tongue to refuse his help and pack him off to the couch, but he's not me, so I give him things to do until our nursery dinner is ready.

We take our plates to the couch. I open the back door and the cat strolls in, sniffing the sausage-scented air.

I've been the victim of his drive-by swipes too many times to let that shit slide. I move my foot to nudge him out, but Ludo's frown stops me. "He'll jump you," I warn.

Ludo shrugs. "I don't mind."

The cat wins, and he beats me to the couch, settling into my spot as though he's been there all along. He leans against Ludo and nudges the hand holding his fork. It's sweet, but I know what's coming. Still. At least it's not my dinner under attack.

We eat in companionable silence. I've overcooked the chips, but Ludo doesn't seem to mind. He makes thick sandwiches, dripping with butter and ketchup, and eats every crumb.

"God, that was good." He flops back on the couch, rubbing his stomach. He's saved a tiny sausage morsel for the cat and holds it out. "Is it yours?"

"The cat?" I shove my last bite into my mouth. "Hell no. Little shit just comes in every day begging."

"But you have cat food in your cupboard."

"He's very efficient."

"Oh wow." Ludo grins as wide as I've ever seen him. "You *are* way nicer than you think."

"Shut up."

Ludo yawns. "I might have to. You've put me in a food coma."

"It's about my turn, but don't go to sleep yet. I've got something for you."

I take the plates to the kitchen and fish a plastic pot from the back of my fridge. It's the most ridiculous thing, but I wasn't able to leave the shop without buying it, a state of affairs I usually reserve for Stella Artois. I return to the couch and hold it out. "Here you go."

Ludo sits up and plucks the pot from my hand. "Fudge flavour? That's amazing. Where did you find it?"

"In the offie. They get random shit in sometimes. Surplus stock, I reckon, not like all that fancy pants avocado stuff you get at the co-op."

"I've never bought an avocado in my life, and I only go to that shop because it's closest to my house." Ludo shoots me a faux glare and tears the yoghurt pot open. "I can't believe you remembered."

I don't tell him that I held an actual conversation with crazy-pen-lid man across the aisle to secure the pot I gave him in hospital. Smiling, I watch him eat, much like I did then, but it's different this time because he's in my house. He's with me because he wants to be, not because we've been forced together by blood and pain.

You morbid fucker.

Not on purpose.

Ludo finishes the yoghurt and gets up to throw the pot in the bin. When he comes back, he surprises me by sliding closer on the couch than he was before. His thigh touches mine, and he leans on me, eyes closed, his limbs liquid.

"I'm so tired," he says. "I could fall asleep right here."

I drop a cautious arm around him. "Don't let me stop you."

"I have to get back for Bella."

"How about a little nod? I'll wake you up in a bit and walk you home."

Ludo makes a sound I take as consent and presses tighter against me. I hold him close as the cat that isn't my cat looks on and wonder if I'm dreaming.

Ludo

I wake up with a crick in my neck, and three things strike me all at once.

One: my chest isn't gripped with the crippling anxiety I usually wake with. Two: I'm not at home. Three: despite his promise to wake me up and walk me home, Aidan is fast asleep.

With Bella on my mind, I check the time and relief washes over me as I realise it's not that late. That despite feeling as though I've been asleep in Aidan's arms my whole life, it's actually only been an hour.

I disentangle us but don't go far. Can't, because I'm enraptured: I can't take my eyes off him. I stare at Aidan all the time but rarely without being caught. With him fast asleep, head tipped back, features smooth, I take my fill of him, undisturbed.

God, he's beautiful. Even his imperfections make my head spin. I trace his jaw with my fingertip and then the jagged scar along my own. Usually, it's enough to ground me, to remind me of my place in the world, but in the peaceful darkness of Aidan's quiet bedsit, I don't care for the dingy hole I dug for myself so many years ago. I don't care about anything except how it feels to be this close to him.

I touch him again, dragging my thumb over his cheek, and cupping his face in my steady hand. Cos that's the other thing about being with Aidan—I don't shake.

One hand is joined by the other, and before long I'm tangling my fingers in his hair, willing him to wake up so I can lose myself in his stormy gaze. Or maybe that's where I'll find myself. Either way, there's nowhere I'd rather be.

"Aidan."

I whisper, but somehow he hears me. He stirs and my name is on his lips as he opens his eyes.

"Ludo."

I bite my lip as he acclimatises to me leaning over him on his couch, invading his personal space without invitation, but as I open my mouth to apologise and shift to back up, he seizes my wrists and pulls me on top of him.

He's broader than me, and my battered bones creak as I straddle him, but we fit together. I press my forehead against his and he wraps his arms around me. I want him to kiss me, but instinct tells me he won't. That if I want this, I need to reach out and take it.

My hands find his face again. I kiss him, but it's not the same. Our lips meet and stars explode, as though all the sweetness that's come before has been used up. The scruff on his face scrapes my skin, and the roughness heats my blood. I clutch at him and kiss him harder. Aidan groans. A sound escapes me too, but I'm so far gone I don't catch it.

He's wearing too many clothes.

The errant thought strikes a match under the desire I've carried for so long. I twist my fingers into his T-shirt. My thumbs graze the heated skin of his abdomen and all I can think of is stripping him bare so I can feel him all over me.

Aidan slips his tongue into my mouth. I go limp and cognitive function abandons me. For long moments my world is narrowed to the slippery velvet invading my mouth and the sparks of magic it sets off in my soul.

"Whoa." Aidan's voice is rougher than ever as he pulls away. "We better stop this shit before it gets out of control."

He's not out of control. He's riled up, flushed and breathing hard, but there's caution too—something I'm grateful for despite the fact that every fibre of my being is screaming at him to throw me down and—

"Ludo."

There's no question in the way he says my name. He isn't asking me if I'm okay, and I'm thankful for that too. So much of my life is wasted checking and testing my emotions. Right now I don't need that. I just need him to keep gazing at me like I'm his most precious thing. "I should probably go home."

He nods. "I'll walk you."

"You don't have to do that."

"I want to."

I have no argument. We leave the bedsit. Cool evening air hits me and the razor-sharp edges of the inferno we started on his couch soften a little. I want to take his hand, but I don't know if he's into queer PDAs, so I don't, and we walk side-by-side, elbows bumping every other step until he slips an arm around me.

We reach my house far too soon. I open my mouth to invite him in. He silences me with a slow kiss, backing me against my front door.

My street is well lit and full of neighbours with twitching curtains, but it's clear Aidan doesn't care, so I don't either, and I kiss him, and kiss him, and kiss him, cursing the fact that the oxygen in my lungs is finite.

I run out of air and pull back. "I—"

Aidan taps a finger to my lips. "Call me soon."

And then he's gone, limping into the shadows and taking another slice of my heart with him.

NINETEEN

Aidan

I lean across the table. "What's a tagine when it's at home?"

Doreen, Bernard's wife, spares me a glance. "Stew, Aidan. Moroccan stew."

"Oh." I turn back to my computer, considering the possibility that she might be winding me up. In the all-female office, I've somehow become the butt of every joke, and half the time I don't even realise until I get home.

Still, Google is my friend. I type *tagine* into the search bar and discover that it's actually the cooking pot, not the contents, and it's weird as fuck. I skim the article and click through to the kind of recipe Doreen, Brenda, and Janet are discussing over tea and biscuits while I sit in the corner like a naughty child.

Chicken, olives, apricots, tomatoes . . . Ludo would love this.

And at the bottom of the recipe it says I can cook it in a bog-standard pan and stick it in the oven. *Winner.*

I take a picture of the screen with my phone and save it for later. Cooking ain't my thing, but since the night I presented Ludo with a plate of burnt sausages and oven chips, I haven't been able to get his answering smile out of my head. It was light and happy and warm and such a perfect reflection of how I feel every time he cooks for me that I can't wait to replicate it. Shame my terrible kitchen skills are holding me back though. If I fuck it up, it'll be funny, and if there's anything in the world more intoxicating than Ludo's smile, it's his laughter.

The day drags on. It's been forty-eight hours since I walked Ludo home from my place, since he kissed me every which way possible, and my craving for him hit an all-time high. We text every hour or so, but by the time five o'clock rolls round, he's fallen silent.

Worry niggles me. I've told myself a hundred times to give him the space and time to deal with however he feels about me. That if he feels even half of what I feel for him, then that's a shit-ton of extra weight on his already overloaded mind. But I don't like it when he stops talking, even if logic tells me he's probably working or napping or old enough not to be tied to his phone all damn day.

"Fancy a pint?"

I frown at Bernard. Somehow I've missed him coming into the office to lock up. "What?"

"Beer, Aidan. Your favourite thing, or at least it used to be. No one's seen you in the pub for weeks. Been drinking alone, 'av' ya? It's not healthy, you know."

My frown deepens to a scowl. "Piss off. I don't drink no more. It's for losers."

I reckon I'd have surprised Bernard more if I'd told him I was pregnant. His grey eyebrows shoot up, and he searches my face, clearly looking for clues that I'm taking the mick. But it's true. Since Ludo found me staggering around outside his house, I haven't been able to catch a glimpse of a beer can without seeing my dad dead on the couch, as though I'm taking making an arse of myself in front of Ludo as a warning sign of what will become of me if I carry on.

Simplistic? Yeah, but it works for me. I'm not drinking because I don't want to, and that can only be good. Plus, getting drunk means forgetting shit, and despite angsting myself into a fucking stroke every ten minutes, I don't want to miss a moment of my life right now.

The sensation of being dropped into the twilight zone is real. I punch Bernard's shoulder and leave the office, my phone burning a hole in my pocket. Ludo hasn't replied to any messages since lunchtime, but I push it from my mind and make my way to the posh supermarket that will have the ingredients I need to make something that isn't scorched freezer food.

I feel out of place the moment I set foot in Waitrose. My first mistake? I'm not wearing tweed, quickly followed up by the fact that I haven't brought my own hessian shopping bag.

Whatever. I'll stuff it down my ripped jeans if I have to.

I trudge up and down the aisles, searching out ingredients and trying not to think about how much they cost. Thanks to Bernard's generosity after the accident and the dosh I'm not wasting down the pub, I'm the most solvent I've been in years, but fretting about money is in my blood.

So much so I'm convinced I'm seeing things when I emerge from the exotic food aisle for the third time to see my cousin Michael perusing the dessert section.

Brilliant. It's been more than a month since he last turned up on my doorstep and weeks since we last spoke. For years I've been a pro at pushing what remains of my family away, of hiding from them and not feeling a scrap of guilt, but since . . . Ludo, apathy has proved harder to come by. Old me would've ducked out of the shop, head down, hands thrust in my pockets, and not given a single fuck. Post-Ludo me grinds to a halt a foot away from my cousin and chews on my lip like a weirdo.

"Uh, hey."

Michael glances up, a box of cream cakes in his hand. "Jesus. What are you doing in here?"

"Why wouldn't I be in here? It ain't just for toffs."

"Yes it is."

"What are you doing in here then?"

Michael grimaces. "It's my wedding anniversary and I forgot, so I'm panic-buying pudding to go with the meal I haven't cooked."

I laugh, can't help it, because it's such a Michael situation for him to be in. Dude is the most diligent fucker known to man, but the flip side is he has so much going on that important shit falls through the cracks. "So what are you having for dinner then? Fish and chips?"

"As if I'm going to get away with that. I've got about three and a half minutes to come up with something amazing or I'm sleeping in the shed."

Michael doesn't deserve to sleep in the shed. He works fifteen-hour days doing fuck knows what six days a week and still finds time to be a decent husband, a good dad, and a far better cousin than I deserve.

I hold out my basket. "Do you know what a tagine is?"

Ludo

Aidan is late. I know this because I've checked the time two thousand times, and it's only Bella sitting calmly at my feet that's keeping me from having a pretty catastrophic overreaction.

Perhaps you should've, like, checked he was coming straight home before you rocked up on his doorstep?

Probably, but my phone is dead, and I've misplaced the charger. I'm hoping Aidan, when he finally gets home, will lend me his.

When. If. When. If. It's not long before the mantra becomes *what if?* But I fight it with all I have because I'm tired of dropping my ridiculous anxieties at Aidan's feet. He's late because he has his own life. He could even be waiting for me at my house. It's not like we made any concrete plans. *What if—*

"I hope you've got grub in those bags."

I jump a mile. Aidan is three feet away, leaning on the wall by his front door, throwing a weary grin my way. "I've got food," I ground out through a tongue that's stuck to the roof of my mouth.

"Good. I had grand plans to cook, but it didn't pan out."

Curious, I get to my feet. "Was it sausages again? Cos that was lush."

"It was burnt."

"It was *lush*. I do get sick of pasta, you know."

"What's in the bags?"

"Penne and twenty tins of tomatoes."

Aidan laughs and rubs his stomach. "Can't wait. Come in."

Bella and I follow him inside. It's natural by now for me to head straight for his kitchen and bustle around as though I own the place. So I do, until he comes up behind me and winds his arms around my waist. He doesn't say anything. Just breathes deeply and kisses the top of my head. And then he's gone, and I hear the shower turn on in his tiny bathroom a scant few feet from the kitchen.

I get the pasta pan out and fill it with water. I put garlic and olive oil in the only other pan Aidan owns and sling it on the hob. But I don't turn the heat on. I stare at it, every sense trained on Aidan in the shower, and I can't move. Don't want to, unless it's to beat down the bathroom door and join him.

Don't.

But *why*? We're not teenagers. We've kissed a hundred times, and I *know* Aidan wants me. It's in every heated stare he sends my way when he thinks I'm not paying attention, every light touch he treats me to, and every lingering kiss that will never, ever be enough.

I want more.

I need more.

My feet seem to move of their own accord and carry me to the bathroom door. It's ajar. I lay my hand on the cool wood, heart thumping, and push it open.

Aidan has his back to the door, the wet outline of his glorious body clearly visible through the translucent shower curtain. He's washing his hair, oblivious to my presence behind him, and I take a step forward, hands gripping the hem of my T-shirt. But doubt hits hard and fast and stops me in my tracks.

What are you actually going to do? Get naked and ambush him? What if—

"Jesus Christ, man. Get in."

For the second time in ten minutes, Aidan startles the hell out of me, blasting a hole in the self-loathing that has me rooted to the spot. Slowly he turns, fixing me with a gaze that even through the curtain draws a heavy breath from my lungs. He lifts his hand and beckons me forward. "Get. In."

"I don't know how."

"Yeah, you do."

His expression doesn't change, and I realise that he doesn't care if I say weird things or get upset about something he doesn't understand. It's . . . freeing. You see, there's a wildness inside me that will never be entirely tamed, and for the first time in forever, I'm okay with that.

I strip my T-shirt and toss it away. My jeans take longer, but with the weight of his stare supporting me, I don't hesitate. He's naked. He has scars. Perhaps we're not that different.

Aidan draws the curtain back. I take his outstretched hand and step into the shower. Hot spray hits my skin. "You like scalding showers too?"

"Uh-huh." Aidan keeps his gaze on mine for a moment, but then it travels lower, roaming my torso. He drags his thumb along the vertical scar on my abdomen. "Spleen?"

"Yeah."

"What about your ankles?"

"I broke them."

"How?"

"I fell."

"On purpose?"

"Maybe."

From the jagged white line on my jaw to the neat surgical scars on my ankles, I see him putting together every mark on my body, adding them into a sum I've never attempted. I wonder what answer he's looking for and if . . . when he finds it, the way he looks at me will change.

Faith tells me it won't.

Fear tells me it surely will.

"Hey." Aidan returns his wandering hands to my face, tilting my chin, forcing me to look at him as water plasters my hair to my cheeks. "We don't have to do anything freaky. It's nice to just . . . see you."

"Nice?"

"Yeah, nice. Don't say it like it's a nasty word."

Nice isn't a term I've ever associated with Aidan, but I try it out for size, absorb how it feels to have his bare skin against mine, his hard length digging into my belly. It's hot but sweet, so . . . yeah, maybe it is nice.

I kiss his chest, then lean back to do my own inventory of scars.

He has more than I thought he would—both angry and neat. I drop to my knees and touch a small gouge mark on his inner thigh. "What happened here?"

"The bone came through."

"Ouch."

"Yep."

"How far did you fall?"

"Far enough to die, but I hit Bernard's van on the way down. Fucked my lung, but I'm still here."

Imagining a world without him is frightening enough to call off my game of chicken with his scars. I don't need to document them to know he's suffered every ounce of pain that I have. More. Because Aidan didn't try to fly, he didn't want to fall, and right now, he wants . . . me.

His cock is inches from my mouth. I should warn him that I'm going to swallow him whole, but I don't, and a shudder—the good kind—runs through me as he staggers back against the tiled wall.

"*Fuck.*" His hands tangle in my sopping wet hair, and he thrusts forward the tiniest amount before he catches himself. "Sorry."

I'm not down with him being sorry for taking the pleasure I want to give him. I work him hard and fast so there can be no doubt of how ready I am to take him apart.

He gasps, quietly at first, as though the turn of events has shocked him, but as I dig blunt nails into his strong legs and scrape my teeth along his dick, gravelly moans fall from him, louder and louder.

"Ludo, I—"

He doesn't need to finish the sentence for me to know he's close to the edge. His legs are trembling, every muscle strained tight, and his breath is short, sharp pants.

I love this. And to know he feels this way because of me is . . .

incredible. I don't want it to end, but I do because I *have* to see the ending. I need it as much as he does.

A strangled sound escapes Aidan. He seizes and comes with a yell, shooting down my throat as beautiful convulsions rock him. Next time I want to be in bed or somewhere without water cascading between us so I can see his face, but there's no time to solidify my plans. Aidan yanks me to my feet, and his hand is around my dick before I can gasp out my surprise.

He has big hands, rough with hard work but a light touch that throws me off balance. I brace myself on the wall, transfixed by the artful way he's working me, how every pull and twist adds sparks of light to my vision.

I screw my eyes shut and then force them open again. This is insane. I've never felt pleasure like it, and I've never wanted it so much from someone. "Oh god, I'm going to come."

Aidan's grip tightens. For a protracted moment, I think I can handle it, but I can't. The dam bursts and I cry out, shatter into a million pieces, and come all over his hand.

White noise fills my ears. I'm dimly aware of Aidan speaking, but not what he's saying. His arms around me make more sense, and I lean into his embrace, burying my face in his chest. I don't know how much time has passed when the hot water runs cold.

Startled *again*, I laugh and duck out of the way as Aidan scrambles to turn it off.

He's laughing too, his so-often-stormy gaze bright with mirth. "I think we fell asleep standing up."

"We should try it lying down some time."

He kisses me. "I'd like that."

TWENTY

Aidan

Ludo stays over. We eat dinner, unfold the sofa bed, and persuade Bella to abandon her stare-down with the cat who's not my cat and join us.

"She left a nose print on the glass," Ludo says, voice heavy.

He's almost asleep, curled against me, naked except for his boxer-briefs. I run a hand through his messy hair. "So? I haven't cleaned those windows, like, ever. One nose print isn't going to make much difference."

"Your cat needs a name."

I can't see how my dirty windows are connected to the nameless cat that doesn't belong to me, but Ludo fades out before he can tell me.

Git.

I spend the next two hours staring at him, missing him, but terrified of waking him up. And of . . . other things. I've never been a good sleeper, but since the accident, I'm lucky if I get more than a few hours at a time. Dreams, if you can call them that. Somehow, I seem to think more when I'm asleep than awake, and I hate it, especially when I wake up shouting, and I don't want to do that when Ludo's here.

Lucky for me, passing the time is easy with him pressed against me. I relive the shower scene a hundred times and then the replay in the bedroom before we had a chance to get our clothes back on. Ludo is . . . fuck, I don't have the words. I've been attracted to him from day one, but I didn't realise how much until today, when his electric mouth blasted every emotion from me but *want.* For those blissful minutes, I wasn't worried about his state of mind, my leg, or where the fuck my life is going. I wasn't worried about anything except how I'd feel when his lips were no longer fused around my cock.

And it wasn't weird after, either. We cooked and ate like we always do, and it seemed as though we've hooked up in the bathroom a thousand times already.

Heat rattles through me at the mere thought of it. My body cries out for me to roll Ludo over and wake him up, but I don't move. It's been a perfect day, I don't need nothing else.

Ludo

I've woken in enough strange beds to not be unduly alarmed when I open my eyes to Aidan's living room ceiling. The fact that Bella is close by—standing over me, actually, jowls dripping with water from the bowl Aidan put out for her—helps.

It's still dark. I suck in a breath and sit up, searching out Aidan. He's next to me, naturally, but he doesn't look as peaceful as I feel. His jaw is tight, his brow scrunched. Wherever his conscience has taken him, he's not enjoying it.

I'm familiar with nightmares, drug-induced and real, and I can recall every time a well-meaning nurse has roused me from one. It doesn't help. Dreams visit you for a reason. Checking out early only prolongs the disquiet. The *what ifs.* So I don't wake Aidan. I leave him alone and slip from the bed to take Bella out for a wee.

Aidan's cat—it's definitely his cat—is waiting on the doorstep. He slips past me and I let him. I'll feed him when I get back.

A quick turn around the block sorts Bella out. We slip back through the door I've left on the latch and I shut it with a quiet click.

But I'm not quiet enough. I turn around and Aidan is awake, sitting bolt upright, eyes wide, shoulders moving a fraction too fast. Despite my best intentions, I've woken him from wherever it was he didn't want to be.

Bella chases the cat into the kitchen, determined to lick him from nose to tail. The cat is fast, though, and more agile than Bella with her clumsy retriever paws. He makes it to the counter in seconds, leaving me to focus on Aidan.

I toe my shoes off and crawl onto the sofa bed. Straddling Aidan is easy. Facing the uncertainty in his eyes is harder, so I don't. I kiss him instead, absorbing his surprised gasp. Then I hug him tight because I don't like it when he's upset.

Aidan hugs me back, his arms vice-like around me. Then he pulls back with a tired half-grin. "I thought you'd left me."

"Nah. Just took Bella out so she didn't take a leak on your carpet. Maurice came in when we left."

"Who?"

"Maurice. Your cat. And don't look at me like that. I gave you every opportunity to give him an Aidan name."

"The fuck is an Aidan name?"

"Like, Butch or something. I heard you calling him Tyson the other day when he was trying to kill you."

"We were boxing. And I won."

"You never win with cats."

Aidan blinks as though the sharp banter has distracted him from being awake and he's only just noticed. "I can't call him Maurice."

"Why not?"

"That was my dad's name."

"And you didn't like him."

"No."

"I don't like mine either." I climb off Aidan and flop onto my back.

He follows me, rolling, so he's leaning over me. "Do you speak to him?"

"Nope. I don't speak to anyone except you."

"What about before me? We haven't known each other very long."

It doesn't feel that way, but I think he knows that already. Perhaps I've told him—I can't remember. "I haven't spoken to my parents for years. They don't . . . understand my bipolar. It embarrasses them. They wish I was like my cousin."

"You've talked about your cousin before."

"Angelo?"

"Yeah. Don't you speak to him either?"

"No." A dark cloud I'm usually adept at dodging threatens the glow I woke up with. "My parents fell out with his parents when we were kids and I never saw him again."

"You never tracked him down? It's not hard to find people these days."

"I've never tried."

"Why not?"

I draw blood from my bottom lip. "By the time social media took over the world, I was knee-deep in a mental crisis I've yet to entirely escape from. There's never been a right time to rock up in his life, and I'm not sure I want to. He's probably living the high life in New York or Paris, and here I am freaking out that there's an odd number of cushions on your couch."

Aidan sighs, deep and long. "There's more to you than bipolar, mate. And there's another cushion over there by the window. I put it there for the cat."

"For Nigel?"

Aidan groans. "I'm not calling the cat Nigel. Why can't you give him a normal name?"

"Define normal."

"I thought you already had by isolating yourself from your cousin."

Touché. "Okay, how about . . . Marcus?"

Aidan shrugs. "I can live with that. Little fucker still ain't my cat though."

Whatever. Aidan can think what he wants, and I'm grateful that he lets me balance tough conversations with banter. It makes them last longer, which means I learn more about him. "So . . . both your parents are dead, right?"

"Yup."

"No siblings?"

"Nope."

"How old were you when your mum died?"

"Six."

Aidan's hair is hanging over his face. I tuck it behind his ears. "So you remember her?"

"Of course I do." He starts to move away but seems to catch himself, as though running from this conversation is a constant bad habit.

Maybe it is.

He starts over. "I do remember her, but not as much as I want to, and it gets harder over time."

I glance around his utilitarian bedsit. "Do you have any photos of her?"

"No."

"Why not?"

"My dad left them in the garage and it got flooded. We lost them all, and pretty much anything else that mattered, but that was my dad all over, useless fucker."

"What was so bad about him?"

Aidan shrugs. "He was a raging pisshead who didn't give a fuck about me or anyone else. I spent my whole life hating him, not realising I was well on my way to becoming him."

He's wrong, of course, because Aidan does care about people. He cares about me, about trees and saving the planet, and about the old man upstairs who can't get to the shops. Not to mention Marcus the cat. But Aidan isn't a man who can be told who he is, so I kiss him again and let it go.

TWENTY-ONE

Ludo

Aidan: *do u fancy a swim?*

I glance at the message, distracted and bemused. The closest swimming pool is seven miles away and probably laced with dysentery. It will take more than Aidan to get me to dip a toe, and that's saying something.

Ludo: *What are you talking about?*

I flip my phone face down and go back to the reality I've spread out on my bed. Pills, *all* the pills, separated into heaping piles that I've counted sixteen times and come up with the same number—two doses too many. *You've skipped days*. But when? I fish out the diary I'm supposed to use to avoid exactly this, but the pages since I started seeing Aidan are mostly blank. It seems that while my head has been full of him, I've let a bunch of things slide.

Angsting, I pack the pills back into their bottles and return them to the drawer. Missing doses of my medication is always dangerous, but never more so than right now—when I'm the closest to happy I've ever been. The little voice in my head has already stepped up a gear: *you don't need drugs, you don't need drugs, you don't need drugs.* Lucky for me I'm presently grounded enough to ignore it, but I have too many scars to believe it will last, and what then?

So it's better to ditch the drugs now and get it over with?

Of course it isn't. Drugs keep me together, and I'm not ashamed. I hate them because I need them, but I love them because they work. Most of the time. If I take them correctly.

Fear is a constant band around my heart, some days tighter than others. When I'm with Aidan, it's as though the elastic has worn out, and I start to dream that it might slip away altogether, but then he goes home—or I do—and the tension returns. Throat aching, I go downstairs and make chamomile tea, but my kitchen, flooded with sunlight from the garden, is too hot for me to contemplate drinking it, so I abandon my mug and take my phone outside.

My garden is unrecognisable from when Aidan started working on it. Gone are the weeds and thistles that previously took up most of the space, and in their place are young herbs and shrubs, tiny and full of promise. He says I can use the stronger herbs—rosemary, bay, and thyme—straight away, but I've yet to pluck a single leaf. I can't, they're too perfect.

I sniff them, though, about ten times a day, more when he's not here. The lemon thyme is my favourite. I rub the bright leaves between my thumb and finger, releasing oil onto my skin, then I retreat to the upturned plant pot that comprises my entire collection of garden furniture and sit on it.

Aidan has replied to my message.

Aidan: *do u trust me?*

Ludo: *Yes.*

Aidan: *are u sure?*

Ludo: *I don't really trust myself, let alone anyone else, but if I was going to trust someone unequivocally, it would be you.*

I send my response and immediately regret how verbose and ridiculous I sound. Aidan doesn't need a twenty-two-word text message to understand what I mean. Sometimes he doesn't need any words at all.

Aidan: *meet me by the gate at 4. bring bella if you want . . . and a towel*

I'm laughing before I know why.

"There's nowhere in these woods I don't know about."

Aidan snorts and grabs my hand. He tugs me through the gate and doesn't let go. We're not exactly strolling hand-in-hand like lovers, but it's close enough that I brave a furtive glance around.

He catches me, naturally. "Are you worried someone might see us?"

"Not especially. I'm more curious how you'd react if they did."

"Why?"

I shrug. "I don't know how out you are."

"Out?"

"As in queer. The only person you ever talk about is Bernard. Does he know?"

"Dunno. But I wouldn't tell him if I had a girlfriend either, so I don't see how that's relevant."

Girlfriend. Does that make me his boyfriend?

Jesus.

I'm not set up for this conversation today, but the dog in me perseveres. "Everyone around here knows I'm queer. I was sleeping with the bloke who worked in the chip shop last summer."

"How does that mean everyone knows? Did you write it on each other's heads?"

"No, he put it on Facebook when I told him I didn't want to see him anymore."

Aidan grunts. "Good job he fucked off back to Scotland."

"You knew him?"

"Vaguely. Before you came along I spent a lot of time in the chip shop."

And the pub. And the working-men's club, hanging out with the blokes from the construction sites in the next town over. It's hard to imagine he was open with any of them about his sexuality.

Aidan trails to a stop and sighs. He fixes two rough fingers under my chin and draws my gaze from the forest floor. "What are you, like, actually trying to ask me? If I'm gay, or if the world knows?"

"The second one."

He snorts. "Well, I *am* gay, and I've never hidden it from anyone. As for who knows, I couldn't tell you, cos I've never cared, but I'm lucky that I can kick the fuck out of any knobhead who squares up to me about it; at least, I used to be able to. That goes a long way in a town like this."

"You've never left?"

"Course I have. I ran off to live with Michael's parents when I was twelve, but they were done with me by the time I was sixteen, and then my dickhead dad got himself terminal liver disease, so I went back to live with him."

"Thought you didn't care?"

"I don't anymore. He's dead."

"Did he know?"

"Yes."

"Was he okay with it?"

"I never asked him."

I never asked my parents if they were okay with me being queer either, but I didn't have to. Their faces when my aunt told them I kissed Angelo on the lips over afternoon calzones were enough.

Aidan sighs again and releases my chin. He rubs his palms up and down my bare arms. "Look, if you're worried I'm going to get embarrassed about being seen with you in public, then you can shut that down now. I'm a private motherfucker, but that's all. I don't care who knows whatever they know about me, and I'll murder anyone who ever gives you shit."

I believe him. Aidan is gentler with me than I deserve, but the beast in him is fierce. I'd only fight him to protect him.

From who? Himself or from you?

Dammit. I shake my head to clear it. "Sorry. It doesn't even matter, I just suddenly had to know, and I couldn't move my feet again until I did."

Aidan's only answer is a slow grin as he pulls me forward, coaxing my feet into motion again. He tosses a stick for Bella, and life, as it always seems to do when we're together, moves on.

TWENTY-TWO

Aidan

Ludo is hilarious. I don't know if he means to be, but he is.

"It's not that cold," I call from the middle of the tiny, secret lake I've brought him to. "Come on."

He shoots me a withering glare and takes another step into the crystal clear water. The late evening sun hits his back, and the glow around him makes him seem like an angel. My angel, cos the thought of anyone else having him has set my blood alight.

Unbidden—and definitely unwelcome—an image of the pale Scottish boy who worked in the chippie last year flashes into my mind. Red-haired and rakish, he caught my eye immediately, but I was working away that summer, a forest project down south. He was gone by the time I returned for good, and I wasn't active enough online to keep in touch.

I picture him with Ludo, long pale limbs entwined, kissing, touching . . . more. It's hot, I can't deny it, but I'm jealous too. So fucking jealous. I'm waist-deep in freezing cold water just to calm myself down.

Ludo scrunches his face and wades in up to his knees. He stands a moment, silent and still, then his face breaks into a soft, glorious smile. "Oh. It's not as cold as it is at the edge. That's weird."

"The sun hits the middle all day in high summer, and it's not that deep, or wide, so it holds the heat."

"So it's warmer where you are."

Ludo seems to speak almost to himself, but I nod anyway and extend my hand. "Come see."

He ventures closer, and my nerves tingle with every step he takes until he's close enough for me to reach out and draw him in.

I feel like I should say something, but I kiss him before words form, soft and slow. He tastes of mint and the lemon sweets he stuffed in his pocket when he rocked up at the gate. I smooth my palms over his sun-warmed skin. It's sticky with clean sweat and then slippery as my hands travel lower. There's a raised scar over his hipbone. I want to ask if he got it when he thought he could fly, but at the same time, where his scars came from has begun to matter less to me. It's not that the details aren't important; it's more that none of it is as important as *him*.

Ludo breaks the kiss and stares at me. He shivers, though I know he's not cold. "How do you know about this place?"

"Grew up around here. I didn't like being at home or around people, but I loved the outdoors, so there's a bunch of secret spots I found over the years."

"Will you show me?"

"Of course."

I want to kiss Ludo some more, but he's so fascinated by the water that I leave him be to wade around and play with Bella while I sit with my feet in the water, smoking the cigarettes I haven't quite managed to give up.

Ludo flicks water at me. I dodge and give him the finger. "Don't start. I haven't had a drink in weeks, and I quit the betting shop months ago. Give me a break."

"Those things will kill you."

"Nah. I'm nearly done with this box and I ain't buying any more."

He doesn't believe me, but there's not much I can do about that except stick to my word. I'm a lot of things, but I'm not a liar.

Or a litter lout. I stub my fag out and tuck the butt back into the box. Then I wade into the water again to wash the stink from my hands. Bella brings me a stick. I toss it for her, and she charges through the water, grinning like a cartoon.

Ludo tips his head back and laughs and I decide that I am totally and ridiculously in love with him.

Ludo

Aidan has brought a picnic. Ham sandwiches with lots of English mustard and salt-and-vinegar crisps. He's even made a sandwich for Bella, minus the mustard, and we eat on the sandy bank of the perfect miniature lake.

After, we lie down and watch the sky change colour. Aidan holds my hand, but he seems distracted, so I shift onto my side to study him. "What's up?"

"Hmm?"

"You're thinking really loudly."

"So why are you asking me what's up if you can hear my thoughts?"

"Because I can only hear the tone, not the actual content."

Aidan's lips twitch. "That so?"

"Uh-huh."

"I'm not going to tell you what I'm thinking about."

I respect his privacy, but curiosity burns bright until it becomes the first lick of paranoia. His eyes are closed. He's not looking at me. *What if he's thinking about someone else?*

My chest tightens, my hands grow numb, and I curse my brain for how fast its negativity can spill out into the rest of me.

Bella rolls over. Her back hits my spine, and the solidity of her down the length of my body is grounding, but it's not enough to halt the lightning-fast shoots of doubt that grow from a single seed.

The sky grows darker and the sunshine takes my mood with it; all the while Aidan dozes next to me, face smooth and free of worry.

I want to hate him.

I can't, because I love him.

TWENTY-THREE

Aidan

"There's a boy waiting outside for you."

I follow Doreen's gaze out of the window and smile. Ludo is tightrope walking along the kerb outside, Bella at his feet, a shopping bag slung over his shoulder. I take that to mean he's cooking, which is fine by me. I've been in the office since six this morning and I spent my lunch break figuring out if my leg is strong enough to climb again.

News flash: it's not, and I'm pissed off, tired, and sore as fuck. Ludo's shower is better than mine. If he's game for a night at his place, I can't wait to wash the day away and pass out in his actual real-life bed.

After some other stuff, of course.

"So?"

"Hmm?"

Doreen nudges me. For some reason, she's decided that shit is okay. "Is he waiting for you? He's been there a while."

"If you don't know if he's waiting for me, why did you say he was?"

"Because I've seen you in the supermarket with him. I wondered if he was your boyfriend."

I give her the coldest look I can muster for a woman who makes me six cups of tea a day and makes extra cheese baps just for me. "How is that any of your business?"

Doreen flushes. "It isn't. I just thought . . . never mind. You're right. I'm sorry, sweetheart."

She backs off and returns to her desk, leaving me torn between making things right and getting to Ludo as quickly as humanly possible. The conflict is real, and the ache in my chest tears me apart as I stomp over to Doreen's desk.

"Sorry for snapping. I didn't mean to be so rude."

She eyes me over her glasses. "That's okay. You just surprised me. Bernard warned us that you were a grumpy bugger, but you've been lovely since you started. I wondered if it was because you had a nice fella."

"It could be because Bernard's the grumpy bugger, not me."

"True, but it takes one to know one, dear."

She's got me there, and I can't deny that her theory is spot on. Ludo *has* chased away my dickhead tendencies. Besides, why waste energy on other people when I can expend it on him?

The thought has me hot all over. I bid Doreen goodbye without confirming her suspicions and leave the office. My phone rings as I descend the steps. It's Michael, but I don't have time for him right now. I cut him off, slip my phone in my pocket, and glance up to find Ludo watching me, gaze sharp, tracking my every step until I'm right in front of him.

I cuff his shoulder. "All right?"

A beat so minute I wonder if I've imagined it passes between us. Ludo's eyes dart to my pocket and back again. "Yup. You?"

His voice carries an edge. I tilt my head sideways, but he's already walking.

I hurry after him. "What's in the bag?"

"Rice. I made some meatballs earlier, but I thought you might be sick of pasta."

"I'm not, but rice sounds good."

"I got some chocolate too."

"Even better." I nudge him and keep nudging him until he looks at me. "You know what I like, right?"

A ghost of a smile lights his face. "I'd hope so by now."

More heat floods me. We haven't fucked . . . yet, but we've spent a lot of time working up to it. By now I reckon he can set me on fire just by looking at me. I don't know how I've managed to get any sleep these last couple of weeks. Not since our slumber parties went nuclear.

And it's every day now. When we first started hanging out at each other's places, Ludo would often step back for a day or so, cool things for reasons I never asked him to explain, but he's different now. He doesn't seem to want to spend a moment apart, and I'm okay with that.

More than okay.

We make it back to his house. I'm limping like a mofo, but I manage to hide it. At least I think I have until Ludo shoves me onto the sofa and presents me with a bag of frozen peas.

"Ice it. I'll make dinner."

I'm still dreaming of his shower, but I take the peas and gingerly lay them over my throbbing knee. The frigid cold does nothing to ease the tension in my muscles, but it's a distraction I desperately need. Sometimes I don't realise how much things hurt until they no longer do. Or something like that.

Ludo brings me a bottle of orange squash and a bag of chocolate bars. I peer inside. "Whoa. You bought the whole shop."

"I couldn't decide which one I wanted."

He says it as though it makes perfect sense to resolve his indecision by clearing the shelf of Mars Bars, Aeros, and Kit Kats. Perhaps to him it does, and something in my mind clicks. I can't remember what it means, but the chocolate seems ominous as I root through it, searching for the Snickers bars.

Ludo disappears into the kitchen. He comes back with crisps and more chocolate before he vanishes again.

I stare at the loot spread out on the coffee table, chewing on the peanut-caramel concoction and willing it to send enough sugar to my brain for me to wake the fuck up. But I don't wake up. I eat the chocolate and some crisps and then my dinner, and then I fall asleep with my half-frozen leg surrounded by mess.

"*Aidan*. Wake up."

"Hmm? Wha—" I jerk awake, half throwing myself off the couch. My elbow bangs the coffee table, sending crisp packets flying, and I curse like a drunk sailor.

Ludo shrinks back. "Shit. Sorry. I thought you wanted to be awake."

"What does that even mean?" I snap, hauling myself upright again.

He stares, eyes wide, and regret hits me like a truck, slamming into my chest and driving all remnants of sleep away. I reach for him, but he evades, and my hands grasp the distance between us.

"*Ludo*."

"What? I said I was sorry."

"You don't have to be sorry. I'm the one who bit your head off."

"I woke you up."

"So? It's fuck o'clock and I'm passed out on your couch. Someone had to."

"I thought you wanted to be awake."

The repetition gives me pause. "Why?"

He shrugs and looks away. I sit up straighter and force his gaze back. "*Why*?"

"You didn't look happy."

It's a simplistic answer that tells me everything and nothing. I try to recall if he pulled me from a dream, but my brain is mush. Without the warning lights of his mood, I have no clue which way is up.

Heartbeats thump. Mine. His. Darkness cloaks us, and I suddenly can't recall how we got here. It's all a blur: the accident, the hospital, even the first time we kissed. I can't remember any of it.

I reach for him again, and this time my hands are rough, *demanding*, and nothing is going to keep me from him.

We tumble from the couch and onto the floor. Thankfully Ludo has thick carpets, but I barely feel the burn of them scraping my skin as I tear at his clothes.

He's not wearing many—just a vest and some sweatpants. No underwear or socks. I lean back and raise a questioning eyebrow.

"I took a shower while you were asleep," he pants out. "And washed up, walked Bella, and—"

"I get the picture." I don't mean to growl at him, but his answering smirk adds more fuel to the fire, and I'm on him again before I can contemplate if manhandling him this way is a good idea. Because it doesn't matter if it's a good idea. For this—for *anything*—to work between us, I have to trust that Ludo will tell me if he doesn't like something. And I do trust him. I trust him almost as much as I want him.

I strip him naked. Then I sit back on my heels as he peels my T-shirt away and runs his thumb over the inch-long scar on my ribs from the chest tube. He frowns, like he always does, and I don't know if he knows he's doing it. Or why. Then I catch sight of the marks on his body; my fingers itch to trace them too. I can't heal him, and I don't want to, but I'd do anything to take away his pain.

"Aidan."

Ludo's whisper startles me. I meet his gaze to find it heated. Hungry. "Yeah?"

"What do you want?"

"What do *you* want?"

He licks his lips. "Everything, but I don't want you to be careful. I don't *need* it. Do you believe me?"

"I believe you."

Ludo grins, but it's more than a smile. It's a smirk that blasts through any imaginary barriers we have left. I stop thinking and shuffle out of my shorts, sending them and my boxers somewhere behind me. A thunk sounds. I've knocked something over, but I don't give a fuck. I'll fix Ludo's place later. Right now, I'm so lost in him the ground could open and I wouldn't notice.

We roll around, fighting for dominance until we realise fucking on the floor isn't going to work.

Ludo leads me upstairs and I tumble him onto his bed. We roll again, and he straddles me, grinding down hard enough to make my vision blur.

"*Fuck.*"

He stops. "Am I hurting you?"

"No, god no. It's not that. It's the fucking opposite."

Ludo presses his palm over my heart, as though he can push the feverish beats back in. He leans down, his mouth so close I can taste his lips without touching him. "Are you sure? Because I'm easy, Aidan. We can do this however you want."

Nothing about my life, including him, has ever been easy, but as I consider his words and what they could mean, I'm happy with that. I hook a hand around the back of his neck and draw him in for a kiss. *I love you.*

He kisses me back. *I love you too.*

At least, that's what he says in my head, and that's how I interpret his every touch as he moves down my body, kissing every mark and scar until he returns to my dick. I wait for him to suck me down, but he doesn't, and I open my eyes to find him leaning over the bed, rummaging in the bedside table.

The arch of his body is so beautiful I don't wonder what he's looking for. His elegant neck and artful spine. His long limbs and slender hips. I try to picture how this might've played out if we met in different circumstances . . . before my accident and the multiple traumas he's been through, but my imagination fails me, cos there's nothing I want more than him as he is right now.

A bottle of lube lands on the bed. Ludo lies down beside me and places it on my chest. "I don't have any condoms, but I got tested a while back, and I haven't been with anyone since."

"I've never had unprotected sex, so I'm probably okay too." The matter-of-factness to my tone makes my words sound far away, as though they belong to someone else, but there's no escaping the renewed tattoo of my pounding heart and the tremble in my hands as I reach for the lube.

Jesus, we're really doing this.

My nerves are amplified by Ludo's silence. But what he doesn't say out loud, he says with his wandering hands. A soft trail of fingertips down my belly, a rough squeeze where I want him most. He brings his lips to my neck and kisses my brain silent again. My body thrums beneath him, and far from overthinking, I can only feel.

We kiss and kiss and kiss, our lips fused as every other muscle and nerve strains to do the same. Ludo rubs lube between us, on me and on him, then he rolls onto his side. His beautiful back calls to me once more, and I fit myself against him. How he knew this would hurt me the least, I have no clue, but as I ease inside him, I feel no pain, only a tight, wet heat that blows my fucking mind.

I knock my forehead between Ludo's shoulder blades and groan. "So good."

He exhales shakily and grips my hand so tight my knuckles crack. "I knew it would be. God, Aidan, I've wanted this for so long."

"How long?"

"I don't know. I-I don't know when it changed."

His answer is the same as mine, and I remember the first time I saw him—*really* saw him, staring at me from across the hospital ward. Despite the mess I was in, fascination hit me like a lightning bolt, building with affection and attraction to where we are now. I can't track the pace. All I truly know is that I'm going to fucking combust if we stay still much longer.

As though he can hear my desperate thoughts, Ludo flexes his hips. The movement is tiny, but it's all the encouragement I need. With the hand he's not clutching in a death grip, I grasp his shoulder and thrust into him. He gasps an unintelligible sound that might be my name, and pleasure rockets through me. The primal need to claim him returns and I dig my nails into the soft juncture of his neck.

It's messy and loud. Ludo meets my every movement with a drive of his own, and the bed begins to shunt against the wall. It's as though I've never done this with anyone. As though every desire I ever had was for him and I saved it up my whole damn life.

I shove him onto his stomach, ignore the creaking protest in my bad leg, and fuck him harder, leaning heavily on him, pushing him into the mattress. He yelps and arches against me. My hands twitch to soothe him. I want to be gentle. I want to be kind. But somehow I know it isn't what he wants.

Ludo makes a strangled sound. "I'm so close."

Relief floods me. And then panic. As ever, I'm fighting a swelling tide, but I don't want this to be over. I ease off a touch, hoping to delay the inevitable, but it has the opposite effect. The change in pace sends new spasms of heat through me, and pleasure coiled deep in my belly sets up an ambush.

Ludo cries out and drives his fist into the bed. His body convulses and the sight of him falling apart catapults me over the edge of the cliff.

I fall like a speeding bullet, and for the first time since the accident, I embrace the world as it zips by. There's no destination. No hard landing. Only a sense of belonging that's wrapped up in something so fucking glorious I can't comprehend it. Sounds fall from my mouth: primal, animalistic shouts that leave my voice ragged, my throat hoarse.

Ludo, Ludo, Ludo.

"Ludo, Ludo, Ludo."

I collapse on top of him. He's laughing and laughing and laughing, and it doesn't occur to me for a single second that such a happy thing could ever be bad.

TWENTY-FOUR

Ludo

I roll over, tangled in bed sheets that need washing. My pillows smell of the woods and Aidan, but I can smell sex too. If I close my eyes, it's as if time has stood still. I can feel Aidan lying over me, moving inside me, breathing beautiful sounds against my skin. With my eyes closed, it's as though he's still here, that dawn didn't happen and he didn't leave my bed to go to that stupid porta-cabin that holds him hostage all day long.

The maniac in me pictures myself creeping out in the dead of night and burning it down so he doesn't ever have to leave me, but I catch the thought before it takes hold. Shake my head and laugh. Despite the fact that I'm all alone, I'm glad telepathy is fictional.

It's early, but restlessness drives me out of bed and downstairs. Aidan has already fed and walked Bella. Tidied the kitchen. Straightened the living room. There's nothing for me to do, so I pace around, thoughts jumping a mile a minute. It's days like this I need a schedule. And I have one, but I've misplaced it, and searching for it only distracts me for so long.

Wash the sheets.

I troop back upstairs and strip the bed. With the sheets bundled in my arms, regret hits me like a stone. I don't want to lose last night, to wash it away. Even if Aidan's coming back tonight, and the night after that, and the night after that, I don't want my bed to ever not smell of him.

So put the sheets back on. But I can't. I've disturbed them now, and they'll never be the same.

I drop the sheets on the floor and flee the room. Downstairs, Bella is in her basket, sleeping off whatever adventure Aidan took her on this morning. Often she sleeps so soundly that I can hoover around her and she doesn't stir, but she raises her head as I thunder down the stairs and lets out a low whine.

"Shh." I bend to fuss her. "Don't start, okay? I'm rattled because I miss him."

Yeah. That's it. Aidan has turned me inside out, and he's not here to put me back together again. Irrationally, I blame him for that. I'm angry. I'm sad. But at the same time, I'm deliriously happy. It's up. It's down.

It's yellow and black.

Aidan fucked me like he loves me. And I love him too.

You should tell him that.

The notion is terrifying, but it won't leave me alone. I tear around the house, searching for my phone. It's nowhere it's supposed to be, but I blame Aidan for that too when I finally find it, half hidden by the clothes he ripped off me last night.

Still naked, I sit on the couch and tap out a text message. Erase it and write another. Words words words, but none of them good enough. In the end I settle for three, and I fire them off into the abyss before I can change my mind.

Ludo: *I love you*

Aidan

Bernard won't stop talking. For the first time since the accident, I've accepted his offer of a pint after work, and this is my punishment.

I want to kill him, but I can't think of a way to do it without seeming like the ungrateful arsehole I am. In my defence, though, I accepted *before* Ludo sent me *that* message, so I can hardly be blamed for wanting to get the fuck out of here and run all the way home to his house.

"So, do you think you'll be fit enough to help with the RSPB project?"

"Huh?"

Bernard's eyebrows dance on his lined face. "The RSPB project. They're setting up the heron station by the quarry, remember? But there's a lot to do before that can happen, and we'll only get it done with all hands on deck."

"All legs, you mean," I retort. "There's nothing wrong with my hands."

"Very funny. How did you get on with your practice climb the other day?"

I search for the words to explain that it was a shit show I had no business attempting just yet, but my brain is so consumed by Ludo that I can only shrug. *He loves me.*

Bernard rolls his eyes. "I liked it better when you had too much to say."

"That's never happened."

"If you say so."

Bernard insists on another pint, even though my glass is still full of the Coke he bought me the first time. He ambles to the bar and I take my chance to fish my phone from my pocket. I open WhatsApp and Ludo's magic message. I haven't replied. I want to, but I can't bring myself to tell him I love him too via a stupid fucking message. I want him to see me when I say it, so he believes me. Because somehow I know it might take more than one attempt to convince him.

I click out of WhatsApp and put my phone back in my pocket. Leaving him with silence seems cruel, but I'm hoping he'll forgive me.

Two pints of Coke later, I leave the pub and let the sugar rush carry me across town to Ludo's house. His house is usually the quiet, messy serenity I need after a day with other people, but as I raise my hand to knock on his front door, I notice two things. One: the door is on the latch. Two: there's music coming from somewhere inside the house.

I push the door open and immediately the scent of disinfectant hits me. It's not quite the harsh, bleach-laced poison they use in the hospital, but there's no mistaking what it is.

Curious, I step over the sofa cushions that are, for some reason, piled on the floor, and poke my head into the kitchen. Ludo is perched on the kitchen counter, surrounded by every pot and pan he owns, bent over his phone.

I knock on the doorframe. "Um, hello?"

His head jerks up and a smile splits his face in half. "Hey. You're late. Everything okay?"

"Yeah, sorry. Bernard dragged me out for a drink."

"A drink?"

"Uh-huh, but I had a Coke. Two Cokes, actually. I think my face is melting."

Ludo laughs. He slides off the counter and throws his arms around me. His embrace is fleeting but fierce, and it's all it takes for me to feel brand new.

I cast another glance around the kitchen. "What are you doing?"

"Cleaning," he says, picking up his phone again. "I couldn't remember how many pots I had, so I got them all out, then I realised the cupboard needed scrubbing, and I couldn't find my Zoflora stash, so I bought some more, and then I found it, so now I have too much."

He stops for breath while I unpick the flood of information he's chucked my way. "The fuck is Zoflora?"

Ludo jerks his head to the left. "Cleaning stuff that kills all the germs and smells nice. It comes in pretty boxes too."

I follow his gaze to a plastic box hiding among his saucepan collection. It's stuffed to the brim with decorated cardboard boxes, all holding small bottles of disinfectant. *Damn.* There must be more than a dozen in there, and *why?* I mean, Ludo's place is clean enough, but he never struck me as particularly diligent when it comes to housekeeping. "What do you want for dinner? I was gonna offer you my terrible cooking, but I don't want to make a mess if you're trying to sort shit out."

"I ordered pizza." Ludo is staring at his phone again. "You can take a shower if you want."

"Um, okay." I back up and retreat to the hallway. "I won't be long."

He doesn't answer, and I troop upstairs, chewing on my lip like he does when he's nervous, still chasing the scent of disinfectant. In the bathroom I find the bath and shower spotlessly clean and the sink still smeared with Cif. I rinse it off and consider the heap of toothbrushes smack bang in the middle of the floor. For the life of me, I can't think of a rational reason for them to be there, but I don't move them. *He's left them here for a reason, right?*

I take the quickest shower known to man and dry off in front of the bathroom mirror before wiping that down too and redressing in my tired jeans. Over the past few weeks, I've amassed a collection of clothes at Ludo's place, but I have no clean T-shirts, so I don't bother. It's too hot anyway.

Eager to get back to Ludo, I hurry to the stairs, but a glance into his bedroom stops me short. When I left this morning, the room was a haven of quiet breathing and sex. Now it seems as though a whirlwind has passed through. The duvet is on the floor and the pillows scattered. Curtains half-open, clothes spilling out of drawers. The bed sheets are in a crumpled heap at my feet. I pick them up, slowly, deliberately, but I can't seem to pull together whatever my brain is trying to tell me.

I pad downstairs. Ludo is no longer in the kitchen, but the pizza has arrived while I've been gone, and two XXL boxes are teetering on a stack of frying pans. I rescue them and take them into the living room, but he's not there either.

Nor is Bella. I set the pizza on the coffee table and check the garden and every other room in the house, but Ludo is nowhere to be found.

Worry licks through me. I call him, but his phone rings in the kitchen. Wherever he is, he's left it behind. *He's walking the dog, dick-head. Don't freak out.* But even as I think it, more anxiety seizes my chest. I rub at it, recalling the many times Ludo has described the physical pain of a panic attack. *Is this how he feels every day?*

A knock at the door rouses me. Spotting Ludo's keys on the back of the couch, I hurry to answer it, but it's not him. It's another pizza deliveryman brandishing two more extra-large pizzas. Bemused, I pat my pockets for my wallet, but the bloke shakes his head. "You paid online."

"Course I did. Thanks."

I shut the door, the pizza boxes warm and soft against my palm as the scent of greasy meat, tomato, and cheese overtakes the lemony-floral cloud coming from the kitchen. Nausea rolls my stomach. All the way here, aside from telling Ludo over and over that I love him too, all I could think of was getting clean, eating dinner, then getting dirty again, but as the second pizza order joins the first, I feel sick to my stomach. Ludo has always been inexplicable to me, but there's something up with this shit.

Something is *wrong*.

TWENTY-FIVE

Ludo

Aidan blinks up at me. "Where are you *going*?"

"To walk Bella. It's morning. Look."

I spring to my feet and open the curtains. Dawn light spills into the room and Aidan shies away, shielding his face. *Oops.* I didn't mean to wake him, but leaving the room without speaking to him seemed impossible. I regret shaking him now, though; he looks like he wants to punch me.

"Ludo, mate," he says, voice growly with sleep. "It's five o'clock in the morning. Bella isn't even awake yet."

I glance at Bella, who, admittedly, is still stretched out in the middle of the bed like a giant hairy starfish. "But it's morning," I repeat. "So I have to walk her."

It makes perfect sense to me, but Aidan is frowning at me as though I've grown horns overnight. I rub my forehead to check and then click my fingers to rouse Bella. "Don't worry. I won't be long."

Bella grumbles and groans. Stretches and rolls off the bed. She's at my feet in moments, and I leave the room before Aidan can say anything else.

He's on my mind as I leave the house though. I'm worried about him—he's been weird ever since I came back from the woods last night. Hovering over me, asking me a bazillion questions about what I'm doing and why I'm doing it. For a man who claims to be introspective and selfish, he's doing a pretty good impression of someone's mother. A good mother, I think. I never had one of those. Maybe he learnt from his own. He's never told me much about her.

The woods are cool and quiet. I take the same route I did last night, but at the fork that would take me to Aidan's tree, I go left instead of right. I've never been this way before. Aidan told me you could walk every day in the woods for a month and not go the same way twice. I'm starting to believe him, and I like exploring. The woods used to scare me, but not today. Today as I tramp through heather and ferns, I feel like I could walk forever.

Aidan

Bernard sighs. "Are you listening to me?"

"Nope." I don't even look at him. Too busy checking WhatsApp every two seconds to see if Ludo has been online.

He hasn't, for the record. Not since he told me he loves me, and as hard as I try to fight the doubt, I'm starting to wonder if he's even aware he sent me those damn-fucking words.

Bernard drifts away. I put my phone down and open Google, tapping in a search for manic symptoms of bipolar. Guilt seeps into every facet of my being, and I feel like I'm betraying Ludo in the worst way possible, but then I picture his wild eyes as he left the house this morning and recall the three hours I waited for him to come back before I had to leave for work. *Nah.* Fuck this shit. Something isn't right.

A bipolar charity FAQ page fills the screen. I scan it from top to bottom, then go back to the start and read it all again with blood roaring in my ears. Every single symptom listed fits Ludo's behaviour over the last few days: over activity, talking too fast, big ideas that go nowhere. Even the bright orange vest he left the house in this morning is a warning sign I didn't understand until now.

I read on to the article written for sufferers, absorb the details and nuances of how Ludo might be feeling right now: euphoric, happy, energised. It doesn't sound so bad, but there's a flip side. A penalty for feeling on top of the world. Wherever Ludo is, he's alone and disconnected from reality. *"It's a lonely place to be,"* the author warns. *"Frightening too, when you realise no one is keeping pace with your racing thoughts."*

A lump forms in my throat. I try to swallow it, but it's stuck, rigid, and I realise it's not going anywhere until I find Ludo and get him some help.

My phone rings on my desk. I jump on it, but it's not Ludo. It's Michael. "I can't talk," I snap. "I'm busy."

"Charming," he retorts. "I'm on my way to work too, as it goes, so I'll only keep you as long as it takes me to get from the train station to the hospital."

"The hospital? What the fuck are you doing there?"

"I work there. Jesus. Are you so self-absorbed that you don't know me at all?"

I am that self-absorbed. As Michael continues to berate me, I realise that I know nothing about his job apart from the fact that it takes him away from his family and makes him miserable. "What do you do at the hospital?"

Michael sighs. "I manage crisis teams. You know all this, Aidan. How do you think I was able to get on your ward at all hours of the day when you were in hospital?"

I've never given it much thought, but I need Michael. I don't know how or why, but with my instincts in overdrive, I'm abruptly certain that he's the only person in the world who can help me.

Ignoring Bernard and Doreen, I shove my chair back and leave the office. Outside I breathe fresh air that does nothing to ease the tightness in my chest. "What kind of crisis teams do you manage? Do you know anything about mental health care?"

Michael's silence tells me I'd have surprised him more if I'd asked him to get me a boob job. After a protracted pause, his voice has lost its irritable edge. "Why do you want to know that? Are you okay? Do you need help with something?"

"Yeah, but it's not for me. I'm, uh, worried about someone."

"Who?"

I ball my free hand into a fist, welcoming the sharp pain from my nails digging into my palm. Clinging to it. "My boyfriend. He's bipolar and I think he's manic."

"What makes you say that?"

I list every sign and symptom I've seen in Ludo. Michael listens and I can almost see his concentrated frown.

"Okay," he says when I'm finally done. "How long have you known him? I mean, it sounds like a manic episode, but if you're not familiar with his behaviour patterns, you might be reading something into nothing."

"It's not nothing," I snap. "Don't patronise me, okay? I'm not a fucking expert, but I know when something's wrong—"

"All right, all right. I'm sorry. I just had to ask. It's not like you've ever mentioned having a boyfriend, so I didn't know how long he's been around."

"Long enough."

"Okay, well listen. If he's been diagnosed with bipolar disorder for a while—"

"He's had it for years."

"Right. So he'll have a crisis care plan. People you can call who are geared up to step in and help for precisely situations like this. Do you know if he has a CPN?"

"Actually, yeah. She's called Rita. That's all I know though. I don't have her number or anything."

"Could you find it? Part of his crisis plan is probably that her details are accessible for whoever's looking after him."

"There isn't anyone like that. He doesn't have any family, and he was alone before me."

"Okay." Michael is quiet a moment. Tapping sounds come down the line, as though he's looking something up on his phone. "Right. I've got some people I can speak to about this at work and maybe get them to call you back. What's his name? And where is he now?"

"His name is Ludo, but I don't know where he is. He went out with the dog this morning and he didn't come back."

"Where would he go with the dog?"

"The woods, I think."

"What mood was he in?"

"I already told you, he's manic as fuck." Desperation is starting to make me dizzy. I find a bus stop and sit in it. "Do you think I should go look for him?"

"If your concern turns out to be founded, then yes. I think you should. Mental health isn't my department, and I don't know much about bipolar disorder, but it's probably best he has someone with him right now."

Michael's right. I know he is. And I'm furious with myself for letting Ludo leave this morning. If I would've gone with him, he'd be safe.

But as I think it, I know it's not true. Ludo was beyond reason this morning. He didn't *want* me with him, and he left the house before I was out of bed on purpose, even if he didn't consciously know it. "I've got to find him, haven't I?"

"Yes, Aidan. I think you do."

Michael hangs up after promising to find someone who actually knows what they're talking about to call me back. He warns me it won't be quick though. *Mental health services are under funded. Even if someone calls you, I don't know if they'll be able to help you beyond some practical advice.*

But practical advice is a world away from the pound-shop knowledge I've claimed from the internet. I'll take it.

I abandon the bus stop, and work, and dash home to give the cat enough food and water to last however long this takes. Then I high-tail it across town to Ludo's house and let myself in with the spare key I stole from the drawer this morning.

Bella is in her basket, a bowl of kibble and fresh water beside her. She's sleeping with her legs in the air, a picture of content, and I tear through the house with my heart in my throat, praying I'll find Ludo as happy as she is, even if it isn't real.

But he's not in the house. I check twice, but he's not here, and his phone is still where it was when I called it last night.

Fuck. My mind races. I chase thoughts down in an attempt to catch every snippet Ludo has ever told me about his condition. What he's been through before and the circumstances leading up to it. But all I can see are his scars on his ankles and abdomen and the chilling words he repeated when he pointed to them. *"I thought I could fly."*

Panic seizes me for real then, and I'm out the door before I can think. I dart across the road as fast as my aching leg will carry me, and the woods envelop me like a nightmare. Vast and empty, even if he's here, it could take me *days* to find him.

I take the routes we've walked together first—the big tree, the lake, the monkey-puzzle grove. The occasional dog walker passes me by, but there's no sign of Ludo. Fear lances my heart as I climb the hill to the railway bridge, but he's not there either.

The secret pond we swam in is my last stop before I lose what little of my mind I have left. I squash ferns and rare heather in my hurry to get to the hidden gate. My clumsiness shatters the tranquil peace of the glade, but I barely notice the birds fleeing the trees or the squirrels scampering away. I burst into the clearing, fully expecting to see Ludo standing by the crystal clear water, wearing the same clothes he wore that day, the same innocent expression of awe and wonder.

But Ludo's not here. Only his shoes are, abandoned at the water's edge.

A silent scream fills my throat.

TWENTY-SIX

Ludo

I find Aidan in the middle of the fairy lake. He's splashing around like a man possessed and I can't help the laughter that gives away my position behind him.

He jumps a mile and whirls around, his crazy gaze taking a moment to settle on me. "Ludo? Is that you?"

I hop down from the tree. "Of course it's me."

He doesn't say anything. Just stares at me, soaking wet, breathing hard. What he's doing looks like fun. I start towards him, but he shouts to stop me.

"No! Stay there. I'm coming."

Well, okay then. I wait at the water's edge. It takes Aidan longer than I expect for him to reach me, and as he emerges from the water, I realise he's limping, like *really* limping, as though he can't put weight on his bad leg. "What happened to you?"

Aidan gets up in my personal space, grasps my chin, and stares down at me so hard it's as if he's splitting me open to see inside me. "Are you okay?"

I duck out of his grip. "Why are you asking me that?"

"Because you've been out all day, you've got no shoes on, and your clothes are all ripped."

"Your clothes are ripped too. And you're the one swimming in your jeans."

"I was looking for you."

"Why?"

"Because I found your shoes and I was worried."

He's not making any sense, and I remember that *I've* been worried about *him* all day. It's why I went for a walk in the first place—to calm myself down. Because everything was too bright and loud and moving way too fast. *Yellow yellow yellow yellow.*

"You should go home," I say. "Get the weight off that leg."

"I'm not going anywhere without you. Come with me . . . come on. We can go to your place and finish cleaning the kitchen. There's loads of leftover pizza."

"What?"

"Pizza," he repeats. "We, uh, bought too much yesterday."

"I don't like pizza."

"Then we'll get something else. Come on, mate. You've been out for hours. Even if you're not hungry, you've got to be thirsty."

I wonder how he knows my tongue is stuck to the roof of my mouth. Then I remember that Aidan is clever and super intuitive. And he knows me because he cares.

You care about him too. If you go with him, you can make sure he rests.

Works for me. I take Aidan's outstretched hand and help him up the slope to the gate. He's moving slow, and when I look at him, his face is as pained as I've ever seen it. "Are you sure you're okay?"

"Just walk, Ludo."

Damn, he's in a mood. Aidan is so sweet with me most of the time I forget that it's not his baseline. I try and keep quiet as we navigate to the path, but it's hard. I feel like we're on a momentous journey, and despite how much pain Aidan is in, I don't understand why he's so cross. "I think we should go on holiday."

"That right?"

"Yeah. Somewhere with waterfalls and stuff. And lots of trees."

"That sounds nice."

"Does it?"

"Yeah."

"Would you come with me then?"

"When are you going?"

Now there's a question. There's an airport ten miles away, but it's a small one, and I don't think the flights it handles go anywhere interesting. "I don't know yet. Maybe tomorrow."

"Uh-huh."

We keep walking. And I keep talking. Aidan doesn't answer me much, but I try to ignore how annoying that is and fill the silence so it doesn't suffocate us.

The gate that takes us to the road appears in front of me. My feet hurt. Aidan hands me my shoes, but I can't figure out why they're not already on my feet.

"I found them by the water," he says. "Maybe you wanted to go for a swim and forgot about it."

"That's ridiculous."

"If you say so."

We reach the road and cross it. Aidan opens my front door and tugs me inside, and instantly the walls of my house feel like a prison. The door shuts behind me and I want to scream. "I don't want to stay here."

"You want to go to my place?"

"No."

"Then you have to stay here."

"Says who?"

"I do. Just have some water, at least, okay? Then if you want to go out again, we'll go wherever you want."

He's not going anywhere. He's leaning on the wall as though it's the only thing keeping him upright, and his gaze is pleading. Desperate. He needs something from me, but I don't know what.

I take a breath. Open my mouth. "Aidan—"

His phone rings. "Hold on," he says and steps right back out of my house again.

Aidan

The woman who phones me is Rita, Ludo's community psychiatric nurse. His key worker. Somehow Michael has tracked her down.

"Where are you now?" she asks. "Where's Ludo?"

"We're at his house. He's somewhere inside, I think, unless he's escaped again."

I tell her about his woodland adventures. She doesn't seem surprised. "Is he hurt? He has been known to get into scrapes and not notice."

"I don't really know," I admit. "I only just got him inside when you called, but he had no shoes on when I found him, and I don't think he's eaten or drunk anything since yesterday."

"Get some water down him if you can. Dehydration will only heighten any delusional thoughts he's having."

Delusional. The word is terrifying, and I still have a lump the size of a small bungalow stuck in my throat. I swallow thickly. "What else should I do?"

"Keep him safe," she says. "I know it's hard when everything he wants right now is probably reckless, if not downright dangerous, but until we can assess him and administer treatment, it's all you can do. Have you been monitoring his medication?"

"What?"

"His medication. It sounds to me as though he might've missed a few doses if his routine has shifted around."

"I—I have no idea. I'm so sorry."

Rita clicks her teeth. "Don't be sorry, Aidan. Ludo is lucky you're with him, and he'll appreciate that as soon as we get him back."

Get him back. Three words that only serve to remind me that right now, Ludo is lost. "When can you assess him? How does that work? Do I need to bring him somewhere?"

"It's probably best if we come to you," Rita says. "He's reacted badly to the clinic before, and if patients are safe at home, we always try to keep them there. A familiar environment is far more comforting than a psychiatric facility."

I close my eyes. "When can you get here?"

"An hour or so. Hang tight, Aidan. I'll get to you as fast as I can."

I have to keep Ludo occupied until Rita gets here, but by the time she ends the call and I go back inside, he's nowhere in sight.

Cursing, I hurry through the house, half expecting to find he's slipped out the back gate and back into the woods, but I find him in the kitchen, rummaging in the freezer.

"There's nothing to eat in here," he says without looking up.

I take a cautious step forward. "Are you hungry?"

"No."

"Then what does it matter?"

It matters a lot. He chewed the crust from a single slice of pizza last night and barely had a sip of water, but I'm terrified of pissing him off. Or making him think he can't trust me.

Ludo shoves the freezer drawer back in and shuts the door with a bang. "It matters because you're hungry, and I can't cook anything decent because the kitchen is such a mess. Why did you get all this stuff out?"

He gestures at the saucepans and baking trays littering the countertop and table. The stacked plates and piles of cutlery. For a moment I honestly think he's joking; then I realise that he has no memory of the chaos I walked into yesterday. "Um . . . we were going to clean the cupboards out, but we didn't get round to finishing. We can do it now if you like?"

"Now?"

"Yeah. Then we can figure out food. There's pizza in the fridge." *So much fucking pizza.* "But we can have something else."

"I don't like pizza."

"Okay, well, let's clean up, then we can sort something else."

Ludo frowns, but his gaze shifts from me to the piles of pots and pans and the open cupboards. "Do you think the saucepans would be better over there?"

"Maybe. Try it."

It's all I have, but for ten whole minutes, it works. Ludo blurs around the kitchen, stashing his things in all the wrong places. When that no longer holds his attention, we move on to the living room and put it back together, albeit in a totally different fashion to the way it was before.

Ludo eyes the sofa. "This looks weird. Do you think I should get a new one?"

Thankfully I'm saved from having to answer by a knock on the front door.

TWENTY-SEVEN

Aidan

Ludo jumps. "Who's that?"

"I don't know, mate. It's your house."

He huffs, clearly irritated, and flounces out of the room to answer the door. If it weren't so terrifying, it'd be cute.

Voices filter out of the hallway. Female, and then the deep tones of a man that ain't Ludo. I tense and take a step, but a woman bustles into the living room before I get any further, towing Ludo behind her, and I drop my fight stance. "Rita?"

She nods. "Aidan. Nice to meet you. Ludo, take a seat, sweetheart."

Ludo pulls a face, his expression a conflicting mix of bemusement, insolence, and affection. "What are you doing here? And why did you bring *him*?"

He jerks his head at the tall man standing by the door, an NHS ID tag hanging around his neck, stance every bit that of someone who means business.

My heart turns over, but Rita merely smiles. "Now, now, Ludo. You know if you miss an appointment and give me reason to be concerned for your welfare, I always have to bring Dr Dennis with me. He's no trouble, though, is he? Give him a break."

Ludo blinks. "Hmm?"

"Never mind." Rita meets my gaze and subtly inclines her head to the door.

I get the hint. She wants me out so she can talk to Ludo on his own. Get his side of the story. I kind of regret tidying the house up now, but I have to have faith that she'll see the same false energy in Ludo that I have. That she'll know what to do to help him, protect him until he comes back to me.

Ludo doesn't notice me leave, he's too busy peeling varnish off the coffee table as I slip past him and into the hallway. Lacking any better ideas, I limp upstairs and finish cleaning the bathroom. Then I retreat to the bedroom and find clean sheets to put on his bed—he wouldn't let me last night. *"You don't like duvet covers. If you did, you'd have one."*

I'm buttoning the pillowcases when Rita comes upstairs.

"I think it's an episode of hypomania," she says. "Do you know if he's missed any medication doses?"

"You asked me that already. I really don't know, I'm sorry. I think he keeps pills in the top drawer of the dresser, though. If that's any help?"

Rita opens the drawer and retrieves medication I've never seen. She shakes a pill bottle and holds it up to the light, frowning. "It's hard to tell when he stores them like this. He used to have a tracker box, but I'm assuming he's lost it."

My leg is throbbing and suddenly feels like it can't hold me up a moment longer. I drop the final pillow on the bed and sit. "I'm sorry, I don't know."

"I don't expect you to know, Aidan." Rita puts the pills back in the drawer and shuts it. "I'm thinking out loud. And I'm glad you're here. Moving forward, it gives me more options."

"What do you mean?"

"Hypomania doesn't last as long as a true manic episode. A few days, usually. If you can stay with Ludo, I'd be more comfortable letting him remain at home."

"Where else would he go?"

"A residential unit, but he'd have to consent or be sectioned, *and* we have the added difficulty that the local facility is full. The nearest bed right now is fifty miles away, and I'd rather not put him through that if we can avoid it."

I'm unfairly surprised that she's even asking me. Not because asking me to stay with Ludo is unreasonable, but because there's no fucking question that I won't. "I can stay. I was going to anyway."

"Why?"

"Because I love him."

Rita nods. "That's what I thought, and I can't tell you how happy that makes me. Ludo is such a sweet soul, he *deserves* to be loved."

"I know."

Rita gives me leaflets and internet links and drills me on what to expect over the next few days. "We've given him an injection to calm him down and a prescription for a few doses of diazepam. Can you get to a pharmacy?"

My leg groans, but I nod. "Yeah."

"Good. If he's been marauding around for a few days, the shot should get him to sleep, but I'd prepare for a crash pretty soon after that. In the meantime, do your best to keep him fed and watered, and clean if you can. It'll be awhile before he's worried about things like that."

I nod slowly. "Is that just him, or is it something that happens to everyone with hypomania?"

"There are some typical symptoms, but I'm quite familiar with Ludo's nuances. He's been stable for quite a while, but blips like this are, unfortunately, inevitable. We just need to keep him safe until it passes."

"I'll keep him safe."

"I know you will."

Rita takes me downstairs and explains what's happening to Ludo. He listens, but I don't think he hears. Already, his lightning fast gaze has slowed, and he's glancing around the living room as though he can't remember where he is.

I move closer to him, within arm's reach if he needs me. After a moment, his arm snakes around my leg and he rests his head against my thigh. I weave my hand into his messy hair and stroke the back of his neck. *I've got you.*

Rita and Dr Dennis—who, to my knowledge, spoke less than three words the entire time he was here—leave. I shut the door behind them and return to the living room.

Ludo is sitting on the floor, still filthy from his forest adventures. "I've fucked it up, haven't I?

"Fucked what up?"

"Everything. I never wanted you to see me like this."

I want to crouch in front of him, but my leg won't play, so I sit on the coffee table instead. "You've seen me with a tube in my chest, throwing chunks all down myself."

"That's different."

"How?"

"You were hurt. It wasn't your fault."

"This isn't your fault, mate."

"It is. I think I missed some lithium doses."

"So? That might've been because you were getting ill and you didn't know. I've got leaflets, and it legit says that can happen in one of them."

I'm deadly fucking serious, but something I've said makes Ludo smile . . . just a touch. A tiny flash of light in the shadows of his haunted face. "Leaflets?"

"Yup."

He blinks slowly. "I feel like I had half an orgasm and I'll never get the rest."

"I don't know what that means."

"It means I like being manic and coming down is the worst thing in the world."

"Injection kicking in?"

"Maybe."

I didn't expect it to happen so soon, and I'm not naïve enough to believe that one shot of sedative will tumble Ludo down from his destructive high, but there's a twisted comfort in watching the energy drain from him. Even if it comes back when the drug wears off, maybe he can rest awhile first.

But before any of that can happen, I need to somehow wash the dirt and grime from his skin. Brush the leaves and twigs from his hair. Dress the blisters on his feet.

"Come on." I hold out my hand. "Let's go upstairs."

I run Ludo a bath and help him undress. He shivers and I shut the bathroom window. The sun has gone down, and the chilly front the weather bloke on the radio has been wittering about all week has moved in.

As ever, my eyes are drawn to the scars on Ludo's skin from the past and the fresh bruises and scrapes from right now, but I try not to contemplate how this could've turned out if he'd been on his own. There's no point—he's *not* on his own, and I don't plan on him ever being again.

"Aidan?"

"Yeah?"

Ludo comes closer and knocks his head against my chest. "Why do you think you're a horrible person?"

"I don't think I'm a horrible person. That takes effort."

"Apathetic, then. Same thing."

"No, it's not. If I was horrible, I'd care enough to be nasty. As it is, I'm nasty by default because I don't care."

"Care about who?"

"Anyone who isn't important to me."

Ludo taps his fingers on my abdomen, a hyperactive rhythm that threatens the odd calm the bathroom seems to have cast on him. I still them with my own and pull back a touch. "I've always found it difficult to get emotional about things that don't directly affect me. And even then, sometimes it's like there's a big black hole where my heart should be."

"Have you always felt like that?"

"No. Michael thinks living with my dad sucked the life out of me."

"Do you agree with him?"

"Not until I met you."

Ludo tilts his head sideways, and I know that even with the kaleidoscope of colours blasting through his mind, he understands. Because he always does. He gets me.

And I've got him.

I coax him into the bath and sit on the floor. He's filthy, but I don't want to wash him unless he really can't—or won't—do it himself. Instead I focus on examining the cuts and bruises littering his body in case he needs actual medical help.

He doesn't as far as I can see, but I can't help imagining what on earth he's been up to in the woods to get in such a mess. So I ask him, naturally, cos I'm sure it's super helpful right now.

Ludo frowns at the grazes on his arms. "I can't remember. I think I've gone a bit magic."

"Magic?"

"Yeah. Manic is magic, baby. Didn't Rita tell you?"

He smiles . . . like, really smiles, and despite my worry for him burning a hole in my gut, I can't help but grin back. "No, she didn't mention it. I googled it, though, and I've got leaflets, remember? Seems like a good time, for a little while, at least."

"It is. Kind of. But it's lonely because no one can keep up, you know?"

"I don't know, Ludo. Tell me."

"You won't understand."

"Do I need to? Or can I just listen?"

That seems to stump him, and he doesn't speak for a while. I give in and reach for a sponge to wash the dirt from his skin, and he pays me no heed as I rub soap over his shoulders and shampoo into his hair.

"Your hair's full of leaves," I say.

He hums. "I think I thought about flying but decided it was easier to roll down the hill."

My heart stills. "Flying."

"Yeah, I went to the railway bridge." Ludo turns in the bath, sloshing water over the side. His cheeks are stained pink from the heat, and his eyes are starting to droop from whatever concoction Rita and her pal have shot into him. "I always go there when I need to remember why I didn't die the last time I jumped from there."

I cup water in my hand and pour it over his head, smoothing the shampoo out. The railway bridge is high and craggy and has been on my horizon for as long as I've been alive. Another fissure in my heart cracks open. "You go there to remember you can't fly?"

"Something like that. I think. I go there a lot when I'm okay, and Rita says I shouldn't go when I'm manic, but I didn't try to fly, Aidan. I didn't want to."

"What did you want?"

He winces. "I can't remember."

"Probably doesn't matter then. Next time, though, why don't you wait for me to come with you? That way we can figure out a way to get down that doesn't get you all dirty."

"I like being dirty."

"I know, mate, but this ain't the good kind."

"Do you still want to do the good kind with me?"

I stare at him, curled up naked in the bath, vulnerable, confused, and trusting me so completely my heart feels like it's gonna fucking explode at any moment. "Always."

"It would be okay if you didn't."

"Well I do, so I don't give a shit what would be okay if I didn't. It's not fucking relevant."

"I need to feed Bella."

"You fed her already."

"When?"

"You brought her home between marathon hikes."

It's Ludo's turn to stare, and I have no idea what he's thinking. What he's feeling. And I hate that most of all—the possibility that he might be scared and I don't know it. That he might need me more than I'll ever know without realising how much I need him too.

I push his wet hair back and squeeze water from the ends. "You told me you loved me yesterday. Do you have any idea how much I love you too?"

TWENTY-EIGHT

Ludo

My bedroom is a nice place to wake up. When the bipolar charity found a tenancy that would suit my needs, they sent an art therapist over to help me decorate. The walls are white, and the ceiling is sky blue. If I'm lucky, when I open my eyes, it gives me a moment to forget whatever chaos I might face elsewhere.

This time, though, I wake with aching limbs and wet cheeks, and I know that somehow, the precious bubble of domestic bliss I've found with Aidan has come to an end.

I roll over with a suffocating sob building in my chest, bracing myself for a cold, empty bed. It isn't the worst thing I've ever woken up to, but it'll hurt the most, and I don't know if I can bear it.

But I'm not alone. My flailing hands touch warm, solid flesh, and the world realigns.

He stayed.

I blink a thousand times. Pinch myself. Make myself bleed. But nothing changes. Aidan is stretched out beside me, face tight with pain, hand clamped on my shoulder, as though he can only sleep if he has me safe in his grasp.

Safe. I turn the word over in my fuzzy head. Try it for size, and it fits. I don't know what I've done to carve worry lines into his rakish face, but with him next to me, I don't feel safe—I *am* safe.

I can't hide from his obvious pain though. I sit up, noting that I'm dressed in boxer shorts and a T-shirt that doesn't belong to me. It's big and black, which seems fitting, but it smells so wonderfully of Aidan that the lingering yellow in my brain prevails.

But my surge of happiness doesn't last long. I lean over Aidan—he's still in the shorts he wears to work and Bernard's company polo shirt—and study his leg. His knee is swollen, as if there's a giant blister under his skin. I touch it, and it seems to pulse beneath my fingertips. Aidan flinches. A sharp sound escapes him, and suddenly he's wide awake.

"I'm sorr—"

Aidan is on me before the sentence completes. He bolts up right with a low growl and snatches my hands as I start to cover my face.

"Look at me," he demands.

I obey, and his stormy gaze bores into me, flaying me open and examining every part of me he can reach.

"How're you doing? Do you feel okay?"

I don't know how to answer that question, so I kiss him, gently, a brush of lips that smooths some of the worry from his face.

He smiles a little, but his intense stare remains. "Talk to me," he whispers. "Can I do anything for you?"

"Like what?"

"I don't know. Whatever you need."

"I need you to be okay."

"I am."

I flick a glance at his inflamed knee. "You're not. And I reckon it's my fault."

"How do you reckon that?"

"You're passed out fully clothed in my bed, and my blood feels like someone spiked it with electricity. There's a needle mark in my arm, and I can't decide if I want to cry or go and have breakfast at that pub that does fry-ups the size of a small bungalow."

I'm wittering by the end of it, speaking so fast I can't catch my breath. It's at odds with the sedative-laced fuzz behind my eyes, and

I hate myself so much I can't catch the fresh tears that roll down my face.

Aidan wipes them away. "The needle mark is from some medicine your, uh, CPN—Rita, yeah, Rita gave you. And there's nothing wrong with crying into your bacon sandwich, if it makes you feel better."

"It doesn't. And I haven't got any bacon."

"Yes, you have. I saw it in the freezer when I was looking for a bag of peas."

"Peas?"

He eyes his leg. "My knee blew up last night."

Something clicks in the tiny part of my consciousness that isn't utterly self-absorbed. I spring from the bed, stumble, and steady myself.

Clearly alarmed, Aidan reaches for me, but I evade him. "I'm fine. Just wobbly. I'm going to make breakfast."

"Ludo—"

"Please. Let me, okay? I need to do something normal."

Aidan clamps his mouth shut. I take my chance and flee the room, and downstairs I find my house neatly rearranged to the point where if I hadn't already lost my mind, I'd be flinging it out of the window.

I open three kitchen cupboards until I find a pan to cook the bacon I've chucked in the microwave to defrost. Two cupboards in search of the plates. The only thing I find on the first try is the olive oil, and that's only because it's still in its spot by the stove.

My thoughts are scattered. It takes me a while to recall that Aidan mentioned a bacon sandwich. *Do I even have bread?*

Apparently I do. I butter six slices and dig out the ketchup. Then, remembering that Aidan's northern, go back for the HP sauce. There's mushrooms in the fridge—*why?*—tomatoes, and eggs. The temptation to cook enough for twenty is strong, but I push it down and make two triple-decker sandwiches, cramming extra bacon into Aidan's as a compromise.

Turn the gas off.

I turn the gas off. Double check it, then unplug the microwave for good measure. *It's safe. Everything's safe.*

Plates balanced in one hand, I leave the kitchen, checking Bella's food and water bowls on my way to the stairs. She's on her back in her basket, tongue out, eyes open just enough to let me know she'll be in the kitchen sharking for scraps the moment my back is turned.

I've left her a rasher on the kitchen table.

Aidan laughs when I tell him so, though he sounds more relieved than amused, as if he's been holding his breath the entire time I've been downstairs. He takes the sandwich with the brown sauce. "Did you turn the gas off?"

"I did. And I checked. Do you think I should check again?"

"Nah. Trust yourself. Never left it on before, have you?"

He's so sweet. And stoic. He eats the sandwich like it's the best meal he's ever had, then gives me a hug, focussed entirely on me and not the throbbing pain I can almost *see* in his knee.

I take the plates downstairs and retrieve a bag of frozen peas from the freezer and a tea towel to wrap them in.

When I get back to the bedroom, Aidan is lying on his back, grimacing, face grey. I drape the makeshift ice pack over his knee and lie down beside him. "Is it really bad? I don't keep painkillers in the house, but I can go out and get you some?"

"It's fine."

"You're a crap liar."

"That ain't a bad thing, mate."

He's right. But his obvious discomfort is getting under my skin. I need to crawl inside his bones and heal the cracks and fissures, but I settle for combing my fingers through his hair while he closes his eyes to the pain racking his leg.

I've had enough broken bones of my own to know how much they can hurt long after the doctors have lost interest. My wrists, my ankles, my pelvis, they all throb in time with Aidan's heartbeat against my palm, and my teeth start to itch. There's nothing I want more than to be the rock for him that he's been for me, but I'm not as strong as him. I'm weak. I watch over Aidan for as long as I can, but by lunchtime the unnatural energy rising in me is irresistible.

My mind jumps so fast I can't catch one thought before it snowballs into another, and I need to *move*, damn it.

"You're vibrating."

I glance down at Aidan. His eyes are closed, but I feel his gaze all over me. "How can you tell?"

"I can feel it. Has the injection they gave you worn off?"

"Yeah, but the mania is wearing off too. I'll be normal soon, I promise."

Aidan's eyes fly open. "Don't say shit like that. As if I'd ever want you to be anything different. And there's nothing abnormal about being ill."

I know that. Of course I do. When I'm well I'd never dream of using such hurtful words about myself or anyone else who has bipolar, but the frustration building in me has spikes, and it makes me say stupid, unfair things I can't take back. "I'm sorry."

Aidan makes one of those low sounds in his throat—the ones that tell me he's either annoyed or horny. Given the context, I'd imagine he's annoyed.

He sits up and pulls the soggy bag of defrosted peas from his knee. "Don't be sorry. You've been looking after me all morning . . . don't you think I want to be *normal* too?"

I concede his point with a shrug. Aidan kisses my cheek, then stands and shuffles to the window. "It's raining."

"So?"

"So . . . we need to go to the pharmacy and get your prescription."

"*We* don't need to do that. I can go on my own."

"I know you can, but I need to feed the cat, so I was hoping you'd come with me. Maybe we can get some ibuprofen too?"

I'm not convinced that he can walk to the end of the road, let alone across town to his bedsit, but Aidan is as stubborn as me when I'm stuck between yellow and black, waiting to fall. He's not going to let me go anywhere without him.

We compromise by getting an Uber into town and going to the pharmacy first. He picks up the smallest pack of painkillers ever. I snatch them out of his hand and put them back on the shelf.

"Jesus Christ. As if six tablets is going to be enough. Get the big pack."

"But—"

"Bollocks!" I snap. "Dude, I'm not going to off myself with your anti-inflammatories, okay? Just get what you need."

I stomp to the cluster of chairs to wait for my name to be called. After a minute Aidan follows me, a slightly larger box in his hand. He drops into the seat beside me.

"Sorry," he says. "I'm not very good at this, am I?"

"Good at what?"

"Being there for you without pissing you off."

"You think it's *you* pissing me off?"

"I don't know what's pissing you off, to be honest, but you're cute as fuck when you're angry."

A genuine, belly-warming laugh bursts out of me. It's so unexpected that I don't know what to do with it. "I'm not cute. I'm a pain in the arse."

"Ain't we all?"

The woman behind the pharmacy counter calls my name. I pluck Aidan's ibuprofen from his hands and go to fetch my prescription. When I come back, he's on his phone, texting furiously.

I've never really seen him text before, unless it's something rude to his boss, and I'm not in the right place to distinguish curiosity from jealousy. I bite my tongue, but naturally he hears my unspoken question anyway.

"My cousin." He holds the phone up. "Turns out he works in some crisis care team at the hospital. He found Rita for me yesterday when I flipped my shit."

"*You* flipped *your* shit?"

"For real. You think I had a fucking clue what to do?"

I have no idea what went down yesterday, and I'm all too aware that my ability to ponder it is manufactured. That if I don't take the pills I have at home and the extras I have clutched in my hand, that I'll regress to that blank space where I simply don't care about myself or anyone else.

Dread fills my heart. I *need* to care about Aidan. About Bella. I can't handle a world where two souls who've given me so much of themselves don't get anything back.

I turn on my heel and go back to the counter. By the till is a display of pill organisers, identical to the several dozen I've owned and lost over the last few years. I buy three. It's not much, but it's a start.

Aidan

Ludo is tired and racked with guilt and anxiety. The diazepam dulls his desperation for frantic activity, but it doesn't dull the pain.

He sits on the couch, curled up in a ball, gaze fixed on a spot on the wall. I bring him all the medication he has in the house and the pill organisers he bought from the pharmacy.

"Come on," I say. "Help me set this up."

"You don't have to do that."

"*Help* me then."

He sighs and leans forward, reaching for the diazepam bottle first while I claim the lithium. "Is this the stuff you didn't want to take in the hospital?"

"Uh-huh. But I don't mind taking it. It's the higher dose I objected to."

"Did they ever lower it?"

"No."

"And what happened?"

"Same as always. It worked and I felt good, so I forgot that I needed it to stay that way."

That makes sense. And it rings true with the million articles I've read online about drug compliance. "You think you'll find it easier to remember if you can see straight away if you've missed a dose of something?"

"Definitely. It won't stop me cycling through being manic and depressed, but it happens less often when I take the pills, and it's less severe. Believe it or not, I think I only missed a couple of doses, and what's going down right now is pretty mild. I've been *way* worse in the past."

I don't want to think about that, but I have to. The bottle in my hand is heavy. I study the label and read Ludo's full name—*Ludovico Giordano*—and try to convince myself that every horrible thing happened to him and not *my* Ludo, but it doesn't work, obviously, cos it's bullshit. "I've got to work tomorrow," I say. "You can come with me if you want?"

"Come with you?"

"Yeah. I'm going to Ashbourne to have a look at some willow trees. They're young and short, so I can assess them without climbing."

I want him to say yes almost more than I want anything else, because the thought of leaving him alone is killing me, and he keeps me waiting a lifetime before he slowly nods his head.

"Okay. I'll come with you."

TWENTY-NINE

Ludo

I like being cold. The chill on my skin distracts me from the sensation of something unwelcome beneath it and my imagination wanders less than it does in the heat of high summer.

Of course, it's still high summer now, but it's *British* summertime, so winter has arrived for a couple of days, and her timing is perfect.

"You can stay in the van," Aidan offers. "I shouldn't be long."

I shake my head. "I like being outside in the cold."

"This is legit the only time I've ever thought you're crazy."

I smile through the diazepam haze. "Works for me."

He parks outside a big house with a sweeping driveway. Paranoia that perhaps he doesn't *want* me to get out of the van licks my consciousness, but ignoring it is easier than I expect. In fact, everything today so far has proved easier than I've braced myself for.

Black is still back, but Aidan's constant presence at my side has lightened the shadows. He brought me breakfast in bed and took a shower with me. Walked me to the shop to get more food for Bella. And he doesn't expect anything from me than whatever I have.

I'm not sure he believed I'd really come with him, though. I don't think he understands that everything he does is fascinating to me. That I want to watch him work.

"Are you fit then?"

"Hmm?"

He rolls his eyes. "Out of the van if you're coming."

I slide out of the van. My ankles twinge as my feet hit concrete, but as ever, I'm okay with that, apart from the fact it reminds me Aidan is still limping. That he couldn't straighten his leg this morning.

We need more peas.

I follow Aidan up the driveway to the door of the big house. A man who's about as far removed from Aidan as it's possible to be answers and ushers us inside. He ignores me entirely, but I don't mind. Observing Aidan trying to hide his impatience for the rich dude's waffle is amusing enough to keep me occupied.

When the man has left us—well, Aidan—to it, he turns to me with a dry grin. "No cuppa. Never get offered one at houses like this."

"Did you really want one? I've never seen you drink tea."

"It's not the tea, it's the humility. If I'd been offered one at the house where I fell, I might've been on the ground drinking it when that truck came round the corner."

But then you wouldn't have met me. And as soon as I think it, a wave of self-loathing hits me so hard I rock on my feet. Am I seriously wishing so much pain and suffering on Aidan just so I got a chance to be with him? To feel this way about someone else when all I truly want is for the earth to swallow me up?

Aidan shakes me. "Whatever you're thinking, stop. Come and look at this."

He tugs me to a nearby weeping willow tree and shows me a handful of leaves. "Willow scab, see? And black canker."

I peer at the dark brown spots marring the delicate leaves. "Does that mean the tree is diseased?"

"Yeah. It has a fungal infection too."

"Will it die?"

Aidan walks around the trunk of the tree and examines more

leaves. His scrunched-up frown is adorable, but I can tell he's worried—and it's different to the concern I've seen painted on his face over the last few days. This I can handle, because I know he has the answer.

"It could die," he says after a protracted pause. "But there's lots we can do to keep it alive."

"Like what?"

"We'll probably start with pruning."

"That's like cutting the toxic bits off, right?"

"Yup."

"Then what?"

"Fungicide treatments. They have to be done regularly, though, or the disease will come right back."

I wonder if he's flinging a metaphor at me on purpose. I doubt it, because he's got that look on his face he always gets when he's talking about trees—the one that takes him away from me for a little while. He walks around the tree again, muttering under his breath, and I'm as captivated by him now as I was when we met, but this time there's no plaster and bandages. No tubes protruding from him and dried blood smearing his skin. This time the pain we share is unseen, and for the first time ever, I feel like I can beat it.

Aidan

I thought he'd be bored watching me trim branches from the sick weeping willow, but Ludo hangs on my every word and even climbs up a few feet and does some of the elbow work for me.

He jumps down, eyes brighter than I've seen them since the first shot of sedatives were pumped in him. And the light is real too. At least, I think it is. Not being able to tell the difference scares the shit out of me.

"Do you want me to go higher?"

"Not without a harness."

I brace myself for him to tell me he doesn't need one, but he nods. "Maybe next time. Do you need to do anything else?"

"Just lecture the toff dude about anti-fungal treatments. After that I'm done for the day."

"So we can get food and go home?"

"If that's what you want."

"Yeah. Can we? I want to cook spaghetti Bolognese."

A silent sigh of relief escapes me. Slowly but surely, he's coming back.

We tidy up and Ludo goes back to the van while I talk to the tree owner. Five minutes later we're on our way home via the Waitrose where I last saw Michael, and I realise I never told Ludo about my abandoned tagine.

I tell him now. He stares at me a moment, as if he's not sure if I'm taking the piss, then he bursts into laughter so infectious that I laugh too.

"I can just picture you stomping around the spice aisle, scowling at everyone, only to give the whole thing away because you're the nicest bloke on the planet."

"I'm not nice." But the retort is automatic and doesn't mean anything. Ludo sees through me. He always has.

After Waitrose—I wait outside—we drop the van back with Bernard, swing by my place to feed the cat, then head back to Ludo's. He's quiet and I'm slow, and I wonder if he's had enough for one day, but the moment his front door shuts behind us, he pushes me against it.

"I want you to fuck me again."

It's the last thing I expected him to say. "Um . . . now?"

"No, not now . . . whenever it happens, but I need you to know that was real, okay? That it wasn't some oversexed manic impulse. If we stick at this, I can't promise that will never happen, but that wasn't it."

I can't deny the relief that floods me. As selfish as it is, the notion that Ludo only wanted me that night because he wanted to make the whole world dance has haunted me in my weaker moments. I've had to stop myself jumping him, just to check he still wants me. "I knew that," I say carefully. "Because you weren't manic when we started this. But it feels good to have you say it. And for the record, we can do it again anytime you like."

Ludo kisses me. It's hot and sweet and permanent, and I know that even if we don't have sex again anytime soon, the invisible cord between us will hold fast. He's stronger than he'll ever believe. He's my harness, and I love him.

EPILOGUE

Aidan

Six months later . . .

Ludo grips the bedframe so hard I'm sure it might splinter. That is if I don't explode into a million pieces first. He's been riding me for what seems like hours, and I can't fucking cope. He does things to me I can't explain, and I'm not cut out for it. I can't deal with the white-hot pleasure sluicing through me or how much I love him.

I screw my eyes shut, thrusting up, chasing the only thing that will end this beautiful torture.

Ludo gasps. He wavers, and I take my chance to overpower him.

I move like a snake and flip him onto his back. He laughs, but I swallow it with a kiss. I drive into him, hunched over him, worshipping him, and I don't stop until wet warmth pulses between us, and I come like a fucking train.

My lungs burn like I've run a marathon. I collapse on top of him and sink a playful bite into his neck.

"Vampire." He shoves me, but it's half-hearted. He likes it when I cover him with my body. It grounds him and helps him feel safe, so naturally I'll lie on him all day if that's what he wants.

It isn't—at least not today. It's early in the morning and winter darkness still cloaks the house, but Ludo's feeling good. He smiles at me, soft and beautiful, and rolls out of bed to clean up and put the kettle on.

I have become dangerously used to weekend breakfasts in bed. Bacon sandwiches, sausage butties, scrambled eggs, and thickly buttered toast—the trouble with being happy is that it might give me a heart attack. I'm not about to turn it down, though. Last week was my first go round at climbing again. I'm tired, sore, and hungry.

Ludo returns with the weird egg thing he does with the rustic bread I buy him from the Italian deli by Bernard's office. He cuts holes in the bread and fries the egg inside it. It's amazing and I can easily eat six of them.

"We're going to Michael's today," Ludo says around a mouthful of food. "I wrapped the presents for the kids while you were in the shower last night. I forgot to tell you.'"

"You didn't have to get his kids presents. He won't be expecting that."

"Yeah, but it's Christmas next week and he'll be expecting you to forget. That's why I stole your debit card . . . so you could pay for them and not feel bad."

I snort out a laugh. "Fair enough. How are you feeling about meeting my tiny family? Are you nervous?"

Ludo shrugs. "Um, not really. Bella's coming, so I'll be fine. I'm a bit embarrassed to meet Michael, though. If he works in the hospital, God knows what he's heard about me."

I recall the one and only conversation I've had with Michael about Ludo since he came through for me six months ago. "*Rita told me he's lovely. That was before she knew I was your cousin, though. Then she told me to do one and mind my own business.*" "I don't think he's heard anything. Rita guards you like a rabid mother hen."

"Probably just as well."

"If you say so. I don't think Michael would ever judge you for being ill. You have no idea how often he stopped me smothering my dad in his sleep."

"I can't tell if you're joking or not."

"Then stop trying. All I'm saying is that Michael's a good bloke. He's way nicer than me."

Ludo takes my empty plate and gives it to the cat—Marcus—who now resides in his house . . . with me. "I don't believe that. You're the nicest person I've ever met."

"Only to you, mate."

He treats me to a smouldering glare. "Liar."

Ludo

Aidan's family—Michael, his wife, and his super cute kids—*are* nicer than him, but only on the surface. I mean, they're lovely people, but there's no one on this planet as selfless as Aidan.

All day I watch him eat the terrible food Michael has cooked as though it's the best thing he's ever eaten, slip sweets to the kids under the table, and repair broken bits of the kitchen when no one's looking, and I realise that no one sees him the way I do because he doesn't want them to. Perhaps if I was a different man, I'd want to fix that, but I don't, because Aidan isn't broken, and neither am I.

In the afternoon, he takes Bella out in the garden with Michael's son to play ball. I stay in front of the fire and play dominoes with the little girl and decide that being warm isn't so bad after all.

Michael sits in a weathered armchair, watching me. There's days that would bother me, but not today. Yellow and black has become a cosy shade of orange.

"You've changed him," Michael says after a while.

I spare him a glance as I try to figure out how to let his daughter win our game without her noticing. "Doubt it. I don't think it's possible for a person to alter the fundamental make up of another."

Michael chuckles softly. "Technically, you're right, but you didn't know Aidan before. I've never seen him so content."

"You don't think he's capable of feeling that way by himself?"

"Of course I do. I'm just glad that he loves you."

I don't understand why Michael didn't say that in the first place rather than coming at me with words that don't mean anything.

Aidan loves me and I love him, but that doesn't mean we've healed each other. Pain is still real. Black is still black. The only difference is that we're both still there at the end.

Still. Damn it. I hate word repetition, and my distraction lets Aidan's niece win the game without any assistance from me. I high five her and wave as Michael takes her upstairs for a bath. It's getting late. We should go soon, but I like being in the bosom of Aidan's family. He belongs here, and maybe I do too.

"What are you thinking so hard about?" Aidan drops onto the floor beside me and stretches out. "Everything okay?"

"Yup. I'm thinking about families. I like yours."

"Uh-huh. Is this a good time to talk about yours then?"

"I don't have one."

"Not true. You have a cousin too, and you asked me to look him up, remember?"

Of course I remember, but I've been hoping Aidan forgot. Tracking Angelo down seemed like a good idea for a hot minute, but then doubts set in. After all, it's not like he's ever come looking for me.

Aidan touches my face. "I don't have to tell you if you don't want me to."

"Tell me what?"

"What I found on Facebook."

"Tell me."

"Are you sure?"

I'm not, but then who's ever truly certain about anything? Knowledge is power, right? And knowing Aidan knows something I don't is a recipe for disaster. "*Tell* me."

"Okay . . . so he's not a dancer anymore, and he lives in Cornwall. He's got a boyfriend called Dylan, walks with crutches, and he does something with horses."

"What?"

Aidan shrugs. "That's all I've got from stalking, and half of my assumptions are probably wrong, but if it's any consolation, he looks happy."

"Is he still beautiful?"

"If you like that sort of thing."

"What do *you* like?"

Aidan grins and kisses the tip of my nose. "I like *you*. But you knew that already. What do you want to do about Angelo? Do you want me to contact him for you?"

That he's willing to speak to anyone who isn't me, Bella, or the cat tells me, as if I ever needed reassurance, that he *really* loves me. I don't know how to answer his question, though. Over the years, Angelo has become an almost mythical being who resides in the darkest parts of my brain. I'm not sure I'm ready to set him free. I shake my head slowly. "Not yet."

Aidan nods and draws his hand from behind his back. His fingers are wrapped around a sprig of mistletoe. "I found this in the garden. Picked it up so Bella wouldn't scoff it."

"Do you want me to kiss you, Aidan?"

His smile is a mile wide. "Yeah, Ludo, I do."

I kiss him. Once, twice, three times. Then I breathe in and kiss him again.

CURIOUS ABOUT ANGELO?

Ludo's cousin, Angelo Giordano, first appeared in Garrett's world in the debut book of the SKINS series, Dream. He goes on to appear in all four SKINS books, along with his gorgeous soulmate, Dylan. Check out the short excerpt below. The SKINS series is available on KU, in print, and now in audio.

Dylan closed the door behind them and leaned back on it, watching as Angelo turned a slow circle in the hallway, his gaze flicking around the mesh of urban and vintage décor.

"This place is nice."

"*This* is the weirdest day ever," Dylan countered, and it truly was. For years, he'd kept most facets of his life separate, but today they'd collided and his brain had caught fire.

"*. . . you did more for me a week ago when I railed you at Lovato's.*"

Was that true? Thinking back over their meeting that morning, it probably was. *Brilliant. So you're a better shag than you are a debt counsellor. Guess Angelo can use a fuck-hot blowjob to pay his overdraft then.*

Dylan shook his head to clear it, struggling to match the Angelo, who'd apparently chucked him all over the basement room mattress, with the exhausted man he'd found in the interview room that morning. Both versions of Angelo Giordano were *gorgeous*, but what had happened in the eight hours since Angelo had dropped his bomb was all kinds of screwed up.

And now Angelo was in Dylan's house. *What the hell do I do now?*

A hundred questions burned on Dylan's tongue, but none seemed right. Water dripped from both of them onto the hardwood floor. Dylan watched the puddles grow until a violent shiver wracked Angelo's slim frame and spurred him into action. "I'll get some towels."

He dashed to the airing cupboard and retrieved two towels, tossing one at Angelo when he returned to the hallway and pointing at the kitchen. "Come through."

Angelo's presence behind him was like a live hand grenade, and the silence that drowned them was too loud. Dylan flicked the switch on his wireless speaker as he passed. The Cooper Temple Clause drifted out, smooth and low, heady and deep, and did nothing to ease the scratchy friction in Dylan's veins.

"The 'Murder Song'? Are you sure it's not you that's the mad axe murderer?"

A dry chuckle caught in Dylan's throat. He opened the fridge and found his last two bottles of Polish lager. "Here. It tastes like piss, but I make lousy coffee."

"I'm sick of coffee. Been brewing it all day."

Dylan had forgotten that. The deli that belonged to Angelo's family made the best paninis in east London, but Dylan couldn't picture him slaving over the press or wrestling with the ancient coffee machines it was famous for.

For better or worse, he could only feel Angelo's hands all over him, gripping him, lifting him while his thick cock drove every last drop of—

"How long have you lived here?"

Dylan blinked and handed Angelo a bottle. "Six months. I lived in Vauxhall for a few years before that."

A small smile fleetingly warmed Angelo's face. "So you weren't around this way for a while then?"

"Um, not as often. Why?"

"Because that explains why we didn't run into each other at the club. I worked there for a year a while back, before I moved to New York."

"I thought you said you hadn't been here since you were fifteen?"

"No, I said I hadn't worked in the deli since I was fifteen. I danced with the English National Ballet for four years—worked at the club for some of that. It kept me out of trouble, believe it or not."

"Get in trouble a lot, do you?"

The ghost of a grin returned, laced with the kind of self-loathing Dylan had often seen in Sam when he talked about his childhood. "I'm not in trouble *now*," Angelo said. "Or am I? You still look pretty pissed off."

Dylan schooled his features. "I'm not pissed off. I'm fucking bemused. Aren't you? What were you thinking when you recognised me this morning? Come to think of it, *how* did you recognise me this morning?"

Angelo licked his lips, his tongue moving slowly . . . sensually as it moistened the skin. Dylan was mesmerised and caught off guard when Angelo answered him.

"It was your voice."

"But we didn't speak at the club."

"Yes, we did. I told you the safe word and you said you wouldn't need it, and then, uh, later . . . you told me your name."

NEWSLETTER

For the most up to date news and free books, subscribe to my newsletter HERE.

This is a zero spam zone. Maximum number of emails you will receive is one per month.

PATREON

Not ready to let go of Aidan and Ludo? Or looking for sneak peeks at future books in the series? Alternative POVs, outtakes, and missing moments from **all** Garrett's books can be found on her Patreon site. Misfits, Slide, Strays…the works. Because you know what? Garrett wasn't ready to let her boys go either.

Pledges start from as little as $2, and all content is available at the lowest tier.

ABOUT GARRETT LEIGH

Bonus Material available for all books on Garrett's Patreon account. Includes short stories from Misfits, Slide, Strays, What Remains, Dream, and much more. Sign up here: https://www.patreon.com/garrettleigh

Facebook Fan Group, Garrett's Den... https://www.facebook.com/groups/garre...

Garrett Leigh is an award-winning British writer, cover artist, and book designer. Her debut novel, Slide, won Best Bisexual Debut at the 2014 Rainbow Book Awards, and her polyamorous novel, Misfits was a finalist in the 2016 LAMBDA awards, and was again a finalist in 2017 with Rented Heart.

In 2017, she won the EPIC award in contemporary romance with her military novel, Between Ghosts, and the contemporary romance category in the Bisexual Book Awards with her novel What Remains.

When not writing, Garrett can generally be found procrastinating on Twitter, cooking up a storm, or sitting on her behind doing as little as possible, all the while shouting at her menagerie of children and animals and attempting to tame her unruly and wonderful FOX.

Garrett is also an award winning cover artist, taking the silver medal at the Benjamin Franklin Book Awards in 2016. She designs for various publishing houses and independent authors at blackjazzdesign.com, and co-owns the specialist stock site moonstockphotography.com

Connect with Garrett
www.garrettleigh.com

ALSO BY GARRETT LEIGH

Lucky

Cash

Jude

Slide

Rare

Circle

Misfits

Strays

Dream

Whisper

Believe

Crossroads

Bullet

Bones

Bold

House of Cards

Junkyard Heart

Rented Heart

Soul to Keep

My Mate Jack

Lucky Man

Finding Home

Only Love

Heart

What Remains

What Matters

Between Ghosts

www.ingramcontent.com/pod-product-compliance
Lightning Source LLC
Chambersburg PA
CBHW020610310726
48979CB00008B/1426/J

* 9 7 8 1 9 1 3 2 2 0 0 3 7 *